CURIOSITIES

OF

FLAGELLATION,

A SERIES OF INCIDENTS,

And Facts Collected by an Amateur Flagellant.

Volumes I and II.

BIRCHGROVE PRESS,
MMXV.

Curiosities of Flagellation, a Series of Incidents,
And Facts Collected by an Amateur Flagellant.
Volumes I and II.

© Birchgrove Press
2015

ISBN:
978-0-9923919-1-1

http://www.birchgrovepress.com

Curiosities of Flagellation was written and published by William Lazenby, a major figure in the underground world of Victorian erotica publishing. Five volumes were planned but only two were issued. The first volume was published in 1875 with the second appearing in 1880. Volume one was printed in Brussels; volume two in London. The text of this Birchgrove Press edition is based on an 1891 reprint.

Curiosities of Flagellation

CURIOSITIES

OF

FLAGELLATION,

A SERIES OF INCIDENTS,

And Facts Collected by an Amateur Flagellant.

Volume I.

THE JEWELLER'S HOUSEKEEPER.

BIRCHGROVE PRESS,
MMXV.

TO THE READER.

The following tales speak for themselves, and are many of them founded on facts within the personal knowledge of the author, who trusts that his more experienced readers will excuse the defects of composition of which he is so painfully conscious.

LONDON, Ist Sept. 18..

THE CURIOSITIES OF FLAGELLATION.

I.

MR. Warren, a jeweller in a large way of business near St. Paul's, having been a widower for some years, for a long time has comforted himself in the loving arms of his housekeeper Sarah, the result of which is a young scapegrace, Master Willie, about eleven years old; he has besides, two daughters by his wife, Miss Annie, sixteen, and Alice, fourteen; as beautiful girls as can be met with about Highgate, where their papa has his private residence.

Mr. W— is reputed highly religious and a strict observer of truthfulness, requiring the same from all surrounding him. When he returns from the City in the evening, Sarah, the housekeeper, has first to report how the young people have behaved during the day. Next Mr. W— has an early supper about half-past seven, which he is very particular about, being a great gourmand; he prefers to have it so early in the evening that some time may intervene before he retires to rest. After finishing up with a glass or two of champagne, thus commences the serious business of correction.

Mr. W.—Sarah, where is Willie?

Exit Sarah, returning shortly with the culprit, a fine fat fair boy with blue eyes and a chubby face.

Mr. W.—So, sir, you were seen tying the cat to the garden roller, and then giving her a spiteful beating. You cruel boy to ill-treat a dumb animal! What do you deserve?

Willie.—Oh, sir! dear father, it isn't true! Mrs. Sarah is always getting you to beat the girls or me for something, she's the one that ought to be trounced for telling lies.

Mr. W.—You daring young rascal to accuse my housekeeper. Your own mother too! What a bad young man you will grow up if I don't cut it out of you. There, not another word! Go to my bedroom, I shall be there presently. Send Annie here as you go out. I've a bone to pick with her.

Enter Annie, a fine, grown, buxom girl, her face flushed with indignation, and her eyes dart angry glances at Mrs. Sarah.

Mr. W.—How dare you look so at any one in my presence! Such temper only proves how true the report is against you. I'll cure you of showing your airs in my absence. Either you or Mrs. Sarah must leave the house, indeed! But I must consult first, I fancy. Come to my room as soon as Willie is done with; you shall have a good birching and be finished off with a wet towel for a *coup de grace.* Perhaps after that you will be more careful in what you say, or who you insult.

Annie.—Oh, father! I didn't say anything so bad as that, although I did grumble to myself. Mrs. Sarah is always so cross with me; do, do, forgive me now, and I will beg her pardon.

Mr. W.—No, no, you'll only do it again if you get off this time. Last week she begged you off, now I'll make you respect her.

Mr. W. (pouring out a glass of champagne.)—Take this, Sarah, to brace your nerves, before we begin.

In a few minutes master and housekeeper enter the bedroom, to find Willie seated on a chair with a most determined expression of countenance.

Mr. W.—Now, sir, beg your mother's pardon for accusing her of telling an untruth.

Willie—No, I shan't, I'll die first!

Mr. W.—Sarah, take his breeches down, and lay him flat on his face on the bed. We'll see if his skin is as tough as his spirit.

Willie.—Keep off! (kicking at his mother.)

All the desperate struggles of the victim are hopeless, for assisted by Mr. W—, his mother soon has him prone upon his face on the bed, where he bites the pillow in his impotent rage; and as she bares to sight the rounded globes of his posteriors, and tucks up his shirt above his waist, Mr. W— takes a fine birch from a drawer. "Now, you young monkey," says he, "I'll tame you a bit."

At first his blows are very tenderly and carefully given, as if wishing first to warm himself to the work, and the boy's beautiful bum gradually assumes a rosy tint, then suddenly a fierce stroke makes the boy bound with pain, after which follow several skilfully administered strokes, making the culprit writhe again, and causing red marks on the delicate surface inside his thighs.

The plucky boy, with tears starting in his eyes, grinds his teeth and clenches his fists, but gives not a single cry, as his mother holds him down.

"So, you're not sorry yet," says Mr. W—, whacking away, and making the birch fly in pieces at every stroke, covering the little fellow's bum with weals and marks; "but I've something will tame you."

Stepping to a cupboard at the further end of the large room, he produces a coachman's driving whip, his eyes gloating with pleasure and excitement as he stations himself at a nice distance from the bed, and wielding the whip like a light fly-rod, proceeds to fish for pleasure on the little bottom before him.

Whisk, whisk, whisk! each skilful stroke almost making the blood to start through the tender skin.

The boy's obstinacy seems to make his father furious, and the blood at last actually trickles over his lacerated flesh, when suddenly:

"Oh, my dear boy, you'll kill him! My poor boy what a cruel man!" cries Mrs. Sarah, as she takes him in her arms, smothers him with kisses, and rushes out of the room with him.

Mr. W— wipes the perspiration from his face as he paces the room. "Ah! there's another; she shall feel the birch and towel! I haven't done half enough yet, and you can't hurt bums. They may smart and make them squeak out, but it does them good. Damn the boy though, he's a plucky one; couldn't make him call out. But how it stirs up my blood and makes me feel young and strong!" (putting his hand in his trousers, and adjusting his person). "You mustn't show yourself, old boy, yet, Annie's coming."

In a few moments Mrs. Sarah re-appears with Annie, who has apparently been weeping, for her eyes are red and swollen.

"Oh, father, father, don't degrade me so!" she cries, "and before Mrs. Sarah too, it's monstrous!"

"What's monstrous?" cries Mr. W—. "Your vile conduct has been shocking and its no use appealing to me."

The poor girl had evidently prepared herself for punishment, as she quietly allowed the housekeeper to remove her skirt and single petticoat, then leaning forward over the end of the bed, she herself opens her drawers behind, displaying the beauties of her finely developed buttocks as she tucks up her chemise.

"That won't do," cries Mr. W—. "Sarah, undo the drawers, the birch is no use unless she's well bared."

In a moment Mrs. Sarah, whose eyes seem to sparkle with anticipated pleasure, turns the obnoxious drawers down to her heels, displaying the splendid contour of the firm, delicious flesh, presently to be lacerated by a father's cruel blows.

Mr. W. (feeling his daughter's firm flesh).—Really, Annie, you're getting quite a woman, and ought to behave better; let's hope this will be the last time you will have to be so disgraced.

Annie.—I know its no use pleading for mercy, so please begin, and end this suspense. I can see Mrs. Sarah is delighted to humiliate me.

Mr. W—, who has a fine new birch in his hand, just lays it on the exposed bum, like a skilful swordsman measuring his distance, then—whisk, whisk, whisk! The blows fall lightly at first as he cleverly manages to make more noise than effect, each stroke causing a rosy tint gradually to suffuse the surface of the skin.

After a little of this preliminary dalliance, the tips of the birch seem to find their way between her thighs, each stroke as it increases in force making her writhe and expose to his lascivious gaze the secret charms of his daughter, just covered with a beautiful auburn down, not sufficient to hide the slightly pouting vermillion lips, now inflamed by touches of the cruel birch.

"Oh, oh! I can't stand it, I shall die!" screams the victim.

"Then mind you don't have to be punished again," says Mr. W—, giving some really hard cuts on her buttocks. "You good for nothing girl, only to think what a bad example you set to Alice and Willie."

"Oh, father, father, spare me, have mercy now!" she cries.

"Not yet, it's not half done you good; birching's like a mustard plaster, and must be borne a little while or it's no use," said Mr. W—.

Whack, whack, went the rod in real earnest now, the poor girl's bottom dancing under the strokes, as each descended on the raw looking surface, the scene of many previous conflicts with her father's correcting hand.

Now she no longer sued for mercy, but her bum wriggled under each stroke, and a strange smile came over her face, as she suddenly shut her legs close together, and seemed to faint on the bed.

"I'll soon awake you up," says her father, as he dips the end of a towel in water, and measuring his distance, administers a succession of sharps flicks, same as with a whip, causing most excruciating pain to the patient, who gives a series of heart-rending shrieks, and really faints this time.

"Take her away, Sarah, and come back here," says Mr. W—. "As quick as you can; I'm bursting!"

Mrs. Sarah soon re-appears, to find Mr. W— disrobed, displaying himself in a state of nature, with a rampant pego at least ten inches in length, protruding in front of him.

"Good gracious, sir, what a state you're in after your exertions," says she, "I must try to ease you."

"Well, make haste then, off with your things; I must finish off on you," says Mr. W—.

Without loss of time she mounts on the bed.

"Which way, Mr. W—" says she.

"Oh, on your hands and knees, you take me in further that way, and its so luscious; I can handle your bubbies at the same time, or tickle your clitoris," says he.

So saying, he is on his knees behind her, and putting his priapus at the mark, is at once sheathed to the hilt in the grotto of Venus; his blood is too hot to admit of slow movements, and he begins a furious course, but, alas! he is not a young man, and his efforts exhaust themselves long before the wishes for climax, whilst Mrs. Sarah, who is fat and fair (not forty but thirty-five), is indeed swimming in delight. The sight of the previous flagellations, although one was her own child, has so excited her feelings, that a very few thrusts of his glorious pego make her spend in profusion. The drops run down her thighs, as he works in and out, one, two, three, four times she comes, before he is able to pay his tribute to her charms. At last the climax is reached, and he sinks exhausted by her side.

"Ah, ah" says she, "no young fellow can do it so well as that, they come so soon."

Mr. W—'s languid cock looked very foolish, as she took it in her and kissed it; her passions were thoroughly excited, and she continued toying with King Priapus for some time, till at last, no longer able to restrain herself, she threw herself on him, and took her deity in her mouth to restore his vigour, at the same time straddling over his face for him to gamahuche her. This he did greedily, rolling his tongue round her excited clitoris, and in and out of her rosy slit, till she sank upon him in an overflow of spendings, which he seemed vastly to enjoy; while it had the effect of slightly erecting his pego.

Such an opportunity was not to be lost, so at once springing up, she mounted à la St. George, and stuffed her gentleman into the longing gap. But it was all to no purpose. She wriggled, hugged, and kissed him all in vain; she was not able to retain the limp affair within her.

"Mr. W—" says she, "you're exactly like the gentleman at the theatre with his wife. Don't you know the story?"

"No, dear," says he, "pray tell me?"

"Well, once upon a time, as stories run," she continued, "a lady went with her husband to see the ballet at Drury Lane, and whilst the principal dancer, a most beautiful girl, was executing her *pas seul*, she noticed her husband excitedly feeling in his breeches.

"My dear," says the wife, "what is the matter with you?"

"My God!" said the husband, "how I should like to fuck that girl!"

"What!" says she, "before all the audience?"

"Yes," he replied, "anywhere on the stage."

"But, my dear," says the wife, "you forget what a fool you'd look if they wanted an encore."

"Now, Mr. W—" says Sarah, "after that what do you say to an encore?"

"Impossible, my dear, I'm quite exhausted," says he.

"We'll see about that," says she, giving his backside a tremendous smack, as she jumped off the bed and seized the driving whip. "You cruel old man, you like to whip children and disappoint your housekeeper of her due, do you? but fair play's a jewel. You don't get off so; if it's in you, I'll have it."

"Sarah, Sarah, pray don't," he cried, as the thong of the whip descended in a most scientific manner right upon his pego, "you'll cut him off if you don't mind."

"So much the better, the disappointing beast, to tease a poor woman so," says she. "There, there, there!" touching him up smartly with the whip at each word, and making him writhe on the bed, "you don't like it indeed, as if your feelings ought to be considered; but I know it takes a sharp cut to make you feel through your tough hide," she cried, working herself into a fury. "Ah, my poor little Willie, I'll pay him out for your unmerciful beating! The wretch, to be so cruel to my darling pet! You know, sir, its all your doing, to pander to your vile passions, that I am compelled to report the innocents for punishment. Take that— and that—and that!" (fetching the blood at each stroke, and the sparkle of her eyes too plainly telling the pleasure it gave her to make him smart).

"My God! Sarah, have mercy!" he cried, in agony, "see, see, your delight is ready for you once more," his pego, swelled by the rush of blood to the parts, plainly demonstrating the theory of Dr. Meibomius in his treatise on the use of flagellation.

"Ah, ah!" she cried, "I'll put a little more starch into him first, or he'll make a fool of me again," (throwing aside the whip, she snatched up a fine new birch). "It's no use paying your man in Covent Garden a guinea a dozen for these unless we use them while they are fresh and green, is it?" she cried, as in a very short time she stood gasping for breath, with the worn stump in her hand, contemplating with delight the scene of wreck on his backside.

A short pause ensued, then eagerly taking his grand priapus in her hand, and kissing it with rapture. "My poor dear old boy I'll comfort you now, and give your revenge on my raging pussey."

Mr. W—, all alive once more, is upon her in a moment, and her splendid legs are thrown over his buttocks, as she heaves and meets him at every thrust.

The battle is long and fierce, and Mr. W— very valiantly sustains her bites and kisses, each time she gives down her rapturous discharge of love, till at last he finishes with one grand push to her very vitals, but she, not to be denied, changes her position and rides St. George, till his languid pego slips exhausted from her still unsatisfied cunt.

"There my dear man, you'll sleep the peace of the just, or rather the unjust now. I've taken it all out of you. You won't want any more for a week to come," she said, kissing him, "but I'll just have a look in at the girls to see if there is anything to report, as I fancy there will be after the warming Annie's pussey has had. The birch makes girls think of something else."

II.

WHEN the housekeeper (Mrs. Sarah) conveyed Annie in an insensible state to the apartment where the sisters usually slept, she hurriedly placed the poor girl on the bed, and ordered sister Alice to tenderly apply a warm fomentation of weak Arnica and water to the bruised and raw buttocks.

Alice sets eagerly to work to examine and, if possible, alleviate the damage done. "Oh, Annie," she cries, with tears running down her cheeks as she views the havoc, "how cruel to use you so, my poor sister. Ah! my turn may come again soon."

ANNIE (opening her eyes with a smile).—Alice, dear, how kind you are to me; but cruelly as they beat me; a most pleasant sensation came over me in the middle of it, and I literally fainted in an extacy of delight. Alice, darling, make haste into bed; I feel I must embrace you to my heart, such a strange excitement thrills through my veins. There, I will lay on my belly and cool my poor flayed bum, whilst you remove my things for me, and undress yourself; but make haste, dear.

Alice bathes the wounded parts a little more, and then draws off her sister's boots and silk stockings, leaving exposed a lovely pair of legs and feet, their marble whiteness being finely in contrast with the poor red bottom they belong to; and her legs being wide apart, slightly display the glowing lips of her virgin gap, as she amorously rubs her *mons veneris* on the bed to allay the burning irritation of the part. The younger sister soon puts on Annie's chemise de nuit for her and hastily makes her own toilet for the night; then putting out the light, she springs upon the bed.

Their lips meet in rapturous loving kiss.

"Annie, dear, lie on me," says the younger, "belly to belly, with our night-gowns turned, it is so nice and warm," (putting her hand down). "Oh, how your pussey burns! put it against mine to warm its little sister."

"Oh! Alice, how you tickle, oh—oh—rub there," cries Annie in a hurried whisper; "don't talk so loud that she devil might come in and catch us."

"Oh! Annie, how you rub yourself against me, you almost smash my hand between us; how you straddle over me," said the little one.

Says the elder: "I don't care about the birching now, it has made me feel in such a beautiful, heavenly glow; I seem I want I don't know what. There—oh—there, Alice, darling, rub your finger there—oh—oh—oh—kiss—kiss—ah, I feel I'm all wet, and on your hand too; but I couldn't help it, dear, its delightful."

ALICE.—La, la, how funny! When they flay my poor bum you must do the same to me.

Soon after this the innocents fall asleep, little dreaming of the important secret they are on the brink of discovering, and which a few more such embraces cannot fail to reveal to them.

When Mrs. Sarah enters again, it is to find them locked lovingly in each other's arms; Alice partly under the entwining limbs of her sister, who, even in her sleep, rubs and jerks herself amorously towards her bedfellow.

"So," says Sarah, "you've found the new sensation!" as she carefully draws the sheet over their exposed forms, and withdraws to look after her little Willie, who she finds awake and restless from the smarting of his poor little posteriors.

"Bless you, my darling, 'tis cruel to see you whipped so!" (kissing him), but you shall have a shilling to spend to-morrow."

"Mother, I wouldn't mind if you gave me half-a-crown every time, I don't care, only I can't pee, my little cocky's so stiff!"

Mrs. Sarah, after applying some soothing lotion to that and his little bum, takes him to her bed.

Nearly a fortnight elapses, when one morning Mr. W— quietly hints to the housekeeper the necessity of submitting a further series of reports respecting the children.

In the evening, after the usual aldermanic repast, as soon as the final glasses of wine have disappeared, the housekeeper leads in Miss Alice, saying: "Mr. W—, I have been insulted again, this time by your youngest daughter. I did think better of her, but yesterday I caught her and Willie putting salt between the sheets of my bed; and both tell me its a lie to my face."

"Alice," says Mr. W—, "confess your fault, and beg my housekeeper's pardon, or it will go hard with you."

No answer.

"You're obstinate, then, and must take the consequences. In ten minutes time, in my room," says he.

"Mrs. Sarah," says Mr. W—, "besides your report, Willie has been digging up and doing damage in the garden with his wooden spade again. Bring that spade with him to my room, he was dared ever to do it again, you know."

As Mr. W— enters his room, he orders Alice to assist Mrs. Sarah in preparing the young boy for his punishment, but Willie at once begins, defiantly, to undress himself. They, however, draw him towards the bed, and as his mother pulls down his breeches to his heels, she finds the boy's little pego already as stiff as iron, and hurries him on to the bed for fear the girl should see.

"So, Master Willie," says Mr. W—, advancing with the birch in hand, "So, Master Willie, you like to play tricks with my housekeeper, do you? and help Alice in her mischief? I'll salt you both for that."

"No, I didn't," said the boy.

"And I suppose you never dug up my choice verbenas and geraniums, and planted a radish bed amongst the flowers, eh?" said Mr. W—, measuring the striking distance. Now we'll see."

Whisk! descends a sharp cut, causing the splinters of birch to fly about, and raising deep red marks across the right cheek of his poor little bottom, while the tears start into Willie's eyes as he clenches his fists from the sharps pain. Whisk, whisk, whisk! as the cuts descend on his tender flesh, the tips of the rod reaching round his buttocks almost to his little virile member as he bounds about on the counterpane. Mr. W— begins so roughly as quite to neglect his usual scientific strokes; his eyes continually wander to the tearful face of Alice, as if in anticipation of the treat her flagellation will give him.

The birch is soon worn to a stump, the poor little fellow never uttering a cry, although his backside is cut and wealed and smeared with blood.

"What, no signs of repentance?" says the father, as he throws away the rod and takes up the little wooden spade, "perhaps a few slaps with this will do you good."

Smack, smack, smack, goes the flat wooden surface on the poor boy's bottom, causing intense agony, as is plainly seen by the way the little fellow bites the bedclothes.

"There, there—there, take him away; he's so obstinate I shall kill him!" says the baffled flagellator.

(Exit Mrs. Sarah and Willie.)

"Now, Alice, let's be getting ready by the time Mrs. Sarah is back again; I'm so sorry to have to punish my pet daughter, but it must be done for your good, my dear," remarks Mr. W—, unfastening her dress and exposing a neck and shoulders fit for a Venus.

"Throw that off, my dear," says he. "Now your skirt and petticoats."

And very soon the trembling, blushing, tearful girl, who is dumb as a sheep before her shearers, stands stripped to her chemise and drawers, her fine shaped legs set off by silk stockings and high heeled boots of the latest fashion.

"Now, my girl, courage, and we'll soon begin and get it over," says he, removing her chemise in toto over her head. "Now the drawers; step out as I pull them down." And the fascination of her beautifully formed legs compel him to give a lascivious kiss on the silken calves, as he pretends to pass the drawers over her feet. Then quickly rising, he is feeling and gloating over the splendidly developed buttocks and firm flesh which is always so hard and yet velvety to the touch in young girls.

Enter Mrs. Sarah, with a fine bouquet in her bosom and a small bunch of roses and violets, which she hands to Mr. W—.

"You must be exhausted, sir," she says, "let me inflict the punishment, if you won't forgive her."

"No, no, she's been too obstinate. But don't be too hard with her, Mrs. Sarah, if you think you had better use the rod," says Mr. W— with a wink.

Alice is now secured upon the bed with a strap across the middle of her back. As she leans forward, her feet, wide apart on the floor, are secured by handkerchiefs round each ancle and through rings on the legs of the bedstead.

The female flagellant flourishes her birch as a warning to Mr. W— to stand aside, he being in the act of officiously handling the girl's thighs and buttocks, under pretence of getting her exactly right.

Whisk! goes the rod; as it gives a first gentle cut, suffusing the tender flesh with as rosy tint, each succeeding stroke adding to the redness; now the end of the birch is skilfully made to touch the lips of the yet unfledged grotto of love, just visible with slightly pouting lips, as her bottom springs to the smarting touches.

"Oh! oh! you touch my——," cried the victim.

Whack, whack, whack! the birch descends in determined answer to her cry.

"Ah, ah! you're cutting me to pieces. Oh, oh! I'll beg your pardon, Mrs. Sarah," cries Alice.

"Are you really sorry now, you bad girl?" says Mrs. Sarah. "There—there—there, you'll do it again soon if not well corrected. Now beg my pardon, kiss the stump of the rod, gather up your things and run away, you've got off easily without a broken skin."

Alice.—Indeed, I am sorry, Mrs. Sarah, to have played you tricks, and thank you for not being too hard with me. (Kisses the rod, and vanishes with her clothes in her arms.)

"Now, Sarah," says Mr. W—, "you have not half done your duty to me in letting that saucy hussey off so easily."

"You're so merciless, I'd rather be flogged myself than see you do it," she replied.

"Well, well, you look got up on purpose to be birched this evening, with your low silk dress and bouquet," says he, kissing her and beginning to undress himself, soon revealing himself minus all but stockings and shirt.

"Ah," says Sarah, slyly lifting the front of his shirt, "you're only half a man to-night. What a time it takes you to recover yourself after one of these evening parties with the birch; no, no, not me this time. I'm the schoolmaster to-night, that's why I came prepared with a bouquet and full dress. Now, sir, (taking a fine birch,) kiss the rod and ask me to do it well."

"Don't cut me too hard," he says, kissing the rod, and laying himself forward on the bed.

"One, two, three, four," says the housekeeper, she applies the green twigs. "One, two, three, four! that's how the girls learn their music scale; and I mean to scale your rhinoceros hide for you, Mr. W—."

Whisk—whisk—whisk! Harder and harder the strokes descend, raising long red weals across his loins and posteriors, and causing his large pego to start into life, as some of the smarting cuts reach the tender part of his thighs, just below the scrotum.

"Only to think of using the wooden spade to my poor Willie! I'll give it you sharp, Mr. W—, this time," she says, looking like a fury, her dark eyes flashing with excitement, her lips compressed in a stern expression, as she seems to inhale the fine perfume from the bouquet close under her nose. She looks the very picture of retribution, a fine subject for an artist to paint on canvas; her dark flowing hair, and the round heaving globes of her gloriously developed bosom, only slightly hidden by a fine piece of transparent net. Her active motions as she plies the rod are full of grace, displaying some one or other charm at every change of attitude; the finely moulded plump arm which holds the birch is indeed a special study, the marble whiteness of her skin making a fine contrast to her black silk dress, the latter trimmed with magenta coloured ribbon.

Mr. W—'s eyes beam with pleasurable excitement as he looks over his shoulder at her, the cuts and weals on his backside seem entirely beyond his thoughts, as he wriggles in pleasure on the bed and rolls over on his side as to let her see the fine state of erection and almost bursting state of his swollen purple headed priapus.

"You nasty old man," she cries, "you want to insult me the same as dirty fellows who expose themselves to women in the street, as if I wanted to see such a thing indeed!" (throwing away the old rod and snatching up a monstrous new combination of green twigs, artistically ornamented with red, white, and blue ribbons). "You little thought, sir, what a fine switch I had got ready for you," she continued, raising her dress with her left hand (as if to facilitate her movements), and displaying her lovely legs in flesh coloured silk hose, and the bottom of a finely worked pair of drawers descending to the knees, or a little below. "How do you like that—and that—and that?" she says, dropping her thundering switch on his already damaged buttocks, each blow making him writhe again, as her left hand quite disappears, the Lord knows where.

"Oh, Sarah, Sarah, pray don't, that's such a whacker," cries the poor victim.

"Yes, to whack a whacker like you, it's just the thing, Mr. W—, to let you know how it feels. Oh, oh, how fine to make you beg for mercy; but I'll not spare! One, two, three, four, five, six!" she says, in fury, each cut spoiling the fine rod as much as it does damage to the exposed flesh, now starting with beads of blood at each stroke. "There, that's the last half dozen! and now for my reward (approaching the bed and passing her hand between his thighs), poor boy, how dreadfully swollen and excited it is, let me kiss it. What a thing it must have been when you were young, Mr. W—. And now to want such beatings to make you any use! Your favourite way, I suppose," she said, climbing on the bed all fours, dressed as she was. "Never mind my clothes, I mustn't lose the chance when he's ready."

Mr. W— does not require a second invitation, but follows up so closely that his bow chaser enters her stern port-hole before she is fairly aware he is so close.

"My God, how big you are, you quite take my breath away, but it's so delightfully hot and warm; a woman's thing delights in a hot roll at any time, and especially the first thing in the morning. But you're never good for that now, Mr. W—," she cries, slowly moving her buttocks to his motions, her white flesh, silk stocking, and black dress making a fine contrast to his bronzed, hairy, raw looking bum, her drawers, being all legs and no behind, offer no impediment to view or enjoyment.

"Bother the morning," says Mr. W—, "the present's the time for me. Women are never satisfied like men, if you only felt as languid as I do after the finish you'd be satisfied. But, ah, ah, how nice! you're always spending, never done, and ever ready again; in fact cock, cock, cock is all you think of, and now you've got it in you my dear woman."

"Oh, further, further! push on, dear, what a glorious fellow it is when well up to the mark! I'm swimming in delight. Oh! oh! urr—rr—r—its heavenly," she cries, sinking flat on the bed without dislodging her favourite, whose furious movements so soon re-excite her, that with one heave of her splendid bottom she regains her former position; the big man's weight appearing as nothing to her erotic strength.

Mr. W— pants for breath, as the pace tells, but manfully does his duty, his efforts pumping a copious discharge from her at every stroke, which streams down her thighs on to the counterpane.

"Now, my dear, I'm coming !" he cries, "there, there, I shall die with pleasure! How lusciously you cuddle and nip him in your cunt! Oh, keep close, don't move, its delightful."

His exclamations are cut short by her ladyship, who suddenly twists under him on to her back, and draws him between her legs, where she at once secures her prize for fear of losing him.

"Now, you naughty boy, I know you want to be off, but I shan't let you," she cried, feeling for a birch under the pillow, "I mean to keep you up to your work, sir."

Redoubling her luscious internal pressures on his still stiff pego, and vigorously applying the birch on his sore posteriors, "Faster, sir, faster," she cries, "No, you won't eh! talk of being tired, indeed!" Whack, whish, whack! "that will make you move a little, my boy. Fine thing to feel lazy and shirk your duty when you've excited me so. I'm almost mad with lust. Oh, urr—r—r, shove quick, I could eat him now!" And smothering him with kisses and bites, she goes off in screams of extacy.

The after languor is so long upon her and Mr. Warren so prone with lassitude, that she unconsciously loses her gentleman, who slips from his throbbing prison in a deplorably limp condition.

"You've cheated me at last, have you?" she cries, viewing and handling the now useless thing. "I know it's no use now, so leave you to your repose, poor old fellow, you would if you could, I'm sure (kissing him and retiring to her own room).

"Now I'm alone, my precious dildoe must comfort me. Ah, ah! perhaps before long Annie and Alice will join me in my sport. I must bring it about somehow. Yes, that I will."

III.

SOME little time now passed and it was nearly a fortnight before one evening Mr. Warren again intimated to his housekeeper that he wished for her attendance in his room after supper, to hold a consultation with her about domestic affairs.

Mrs. Sarah's experience told her that the master for once in a way intended to specially honour her bottom by his attentions, so retiring to her room, she presently re-appeared in his apartment attired in a splendid dress of dark blue silk, trimmed with black, but made so low in the neck as to display the development of her bosom, the fascinating whiteness of her skin being set off by a lovely bunch of roses fixed between the swelling globes. Her dark flashing eyes and dimpled smile literally threw out a challenge to him to do his worst.

"Well, I never!" he exclaimed, "you know you are in disgrace for something and yet dare to try and disarm me by appearing as fascinating as possible; but I'll steel my heart to all your blandishments. Now how is it you make no reports about the children as usual, eh?"

"Why, sir, they have been so good lately and besides you beat them so cruelly when you do punish them, that unless it is something serious, I don't like to have them hurt," she replied.

"In fact, Sarah," says Mr. W——, "you think I'm unjust, and so neglect your duty, but you shall smart for it yourself. I've been to Covent Garden today, and bought half-a-dozen extra fine fresh green birches. So now, one smell of your roses, and then to business." With that he drew her on to his lap, put his nose between the hillocks of her bosom, and devoured them with kisses.

"There—there—it grieves me, but you must be made to do your duty. You see I'm ready in my dressing-gown, I've no assistant to help me, so I must prepare you myself."

"Then, then, you won't forgive me? Oh, don't birch your poor Sarah, who serves you so well. I, I'll, do as you want in future," she cries.

"No, no, not now, you're too beautiful. I must make the real tears of repentance flow. You bad woman, I'm deaf to your wiles, now I remember how you cut my poor backside to pieces the last time," he said, eagerly beginning to unloose her dress.

That removed, a tight knot defies his fumbling fingers, as he endeavours to take off the under petticoats of white quilted satin. Like the great Alexander, he is compelled to cut the Gordian knot, and is rewarded by the sight of her shapely hips and thighs, encased in rather tight drawers. Nothing but the tail of her chemise now covers the plump bottom he is hastening to expose, and his hand rapidly passes between her thighs to pull away the obnoxious linen.

"Oh, oh, oh! you spiteful man, as if you couldn't do that without pulling my hair," she screamed.

Slap, slap, slap, went his hand on her flesh, as he pulled away the slight impediment.

"There—there, that's for your noise; you know I didn't do anything of the sort," he exclaimed.

"Oh, you old fibber," she retorted, "you know you did."

"How impudent," says Mr.W—. "You'll come to be a little more truthful presently, you hussey." So saying, he at once drew the drawers down to her heels, making her step clear as he passed them over her boots. While doing so he could not resist caressing her splendid legs and thighs, casting a slyly malicious glance at the rich pouting gap between her legs, so enchantingly fringed with its luxuriant growth of black hair.

She was indeed a sight to warm the feelings of an anchorite. Now her chemise is drawn over her head, and she stands reclining over the foot of the bed, her legs wide apart, and displaying the full development of her glorious buttocks and finely moulded back and shoulders.

Mr. W— gazes in delight, as he poises his ponderous birch for a swoop upon those devoted charms.

"I think, ma'am," says he, "you'll find I've got a regular tickler for you to-day," as he gently whisks the tip towards his victim.

"Now I must begin in earnest, and teach you not to neglect your reports in future," he said.

"Oh! take care, Mr. W—," she says, "I may be in the family way."

"Eh! indeed," he cries, "I'll satisfy your longings then, I think you've a fancy for something this evening, you brazen woman, to come to me dressed as if to go to an evening party. There—there—there," as the great bunch of twigs cuts on the throbbing flesh, each blow changing more and more of the white surface to a pinky hue.

The lecherous old fellow regularly works over the large field of firm and solid flesh upon her buttocks, not forgetting now and then to let the stinging tips of his rod touch up the most tender parts between her thighs; even the hairy grotto of love does not escape, when he sees a chance of a sly cut.

"Oh—oh—ah, you're—! oh! spare my poor pussey," she cries, writhing with the smarting agony.

His eyes flash with pleasure as each cut brings up the weals and marks, making the blood almost start through the skin.

Whack, whack, "there, you lewd woman, do you call that your pussey?" he says, causing the birch, by an underhand stroke, to strike right along her throbbing gap, even to the mount in front.

"Oh—oh, you monster!" she screams, "do have some pity. Ah—ah—you'll kill me altogether!" as his fury increases, and slight drops of blood besmear the now ruby coloured flesh, her cries grow less. A new sensation of a beautiful burning heat comes over her, one hand steals down to an excited clitoris; and with a smile she seems to die away almost insensible on the bed; nothing but slight quivering wriggles answering to each stroke of her flagellator.

"She's cheated me, she's having all the pleasure to herself!" he exclaims, throwing off his dressing-gown, and bringing his now excited pego to the mark.

A copious discharge has well lubricated the smarting grotto, as he finds to his delight by the ready entrance of his enormous affair, which fairly revels in the delicious pressures of the excited vagina. For a few moments he quietly enjoys his position, then gently beginning with a slow in-and-out motion, soon rouses his wanton housekeeper to action.

Her bottom, sore as it is, heaves in response to each exciting thrust, and her lascivious contractions put him into an agony of delight, by the way her greedy cunt clings to his bursting pego.

Almost quicker than it takes to relate, she again comes in a hot boiling spend, so exciting Mr. W— that he pushes on with increased vigour, to her intense delight, making her scream with extacy, as she lies in a continuous discharge of love's essence.

"Oh—oh—oh—uh—r! you dear man," she cries. "I forgive you now for all the birching. Push, push, push on, it's heavenly!"

"Oh, Sarah!" exclaims Mr. W—, "I must come now, I'm bursting. There—oh—there," as he injects the spurting juice of his noble priapus far up into her delighted vitals; and they both sink exhausted on the bed.

For a long time they lay in the after enjoyment of throbs and pressures of cunt and cock, till at last Mr. Warren's limp affair slips away from Mrs. Sarah's still longing gap.

Mr. W— deprecated all idea of renewing the battle, on the plea of weakness, and although the housekeeper knew there was still a good fuck in him if only properly birched, she apparently acquiesced (having another idea of further enjoyment), lovingly wished him pleasant dreams, and retired to her own apartment.

Now the idea of going to bed was far from Mrs. Sarah's thoughts. Even while apparently exhausting her love on Mr. W—, her pleasure was raised to highest pitch by libidinous thoughts of a contemplated visit to Annie and Alice in their room, as soon as she could get away.

The night was still young, not more than ten o'clock, as the two loving sisters were discussing their affairs.

"Ah!" says Alice, twinning the soft auburn curls on her sisters's mount with her finger, "if Mrs. Sarah has as good a crop on her pussey as she ought to have at her age, what a splendid sight it must be! Such beautiful white flesh and glossy black hair!"

"Alice, dear, how you tickle! Do you know I could indeed love Mrs. Sarah, badly as she has treated us, if I could once see her whipped as papa whips us. Isn't it strange? I do so long to see her fine fat bum properly flayed by the birch! What a pity we are not strong enough to do it, you and I; but perhaps when cousin Catherine comes next week, we might persuade her to help us to our revenge. She's so famously strong, you know," said Annie.

"Oh, oh, Annie!" replies Alice, "how dare you think of such a thing. They would whip us to death."

"Never mind about that, I wouldn't care," says the elder sister, "besides, after a little while the beautiful sensation comes over me, my limbs quiver with pleasure, and I feel a something come inside of me, so nice that I almost go off in a faint of extasy, regardless of the birch, and I'm all wet afterwards down there, the same as when you rub and tickle me so nicely, you darling!"

"La! you tickle me too Annie," said the little one.

"My dears, what are you doing to talk so?" cries Mrs. Sarah, who had approached the bed unseen by the now frightened sisters. "Ah, Annie, I must kiss you for saying you could love me. There, there!" (imprinting hot burning kisses on the girl's lips), "won't you kiss me, dear, if I love you both?"

"Yes, oh yes!" (returning kiss for kiss), says the impulsive girl, "if I could but give you a good birching."

"My dear, your papa has already done that for you. You shall soon see how you have been revenged," says the housekeeper.

Then lighting their candles, and fetching two more from her own room, so as to make a good light, she gets on the bed and shows her poor scarred, red bottom to the astonished girls.

"Oh, my gracious! you have caught it sharp!" says Alice.

"How did you feel?"

"My dears, it's awful at first, but soon you begin to feel all hot and warm like on your bottom and between your legs, till at last you seem to faint in pleasure," says Mrs. Sarah.

Annie feels so curious and amorously excited, that as Mrs. Sarah kisses her again, her hand by accident gets caught between the housekeeper's thighs.

"La! how wet and burning hot you feel!" says the girl.

"Ah, my dear, it's the pleasure I've felt," replies Mrs. Sarah.

"I wish there was a birch here," says young Alice.

"What for, my dear?" says the housekeeper.

"I should like you to try if I could feel the same as you describe," says Alice.

"There's two in my room, and you shall birch Annie exactly as I do; my poor bottom is too sore for more to-night. However, Mr. W— is going away for a fortnight, and when cousin Catherine comes we'll have a grand birch soiree," says Mrs. Sarah, tripping off to her room for the rods.

Presently she returns with two nice light birches elegantly bound with blue ribbon, and handing one to Alice, says, "Now, my dears, let's off with every thing before we begin, the weather is so warm.

"Come, Annie, lean over the end of the bed, for Alice to operate on your bottom, whilst I do the same for her little bum, and Alice, begin gently, and do exactly as I do," she continued.

She gently flourishes the rod towards the fair girl's buttocks; the fine dark woman with her dazzling white flesh, and the two fair girls making a most fascinating group. Mrs. Sarah's eyes fairly sparkle with delight as she realises in her mind all the extatic pleasure now at her disposal.

Whisk, whisk, whisk! the strokes gently fall on the hard firm little buttocks, and Alice passes on stroke for stroke, the two fair bottoms assuming first a rosy and then a redder tint, as the blows get heavier.

Mrs. Sarah administers each stroke with clever deliberation, first to the right, then to the left, across the buttocks, then by skilful up-strokes the tender under surfaces are reached, till Alice's little pussey tingles with the warmth of the blood rushing to her private parts.

The rods in use are so slightly made that with moderate force they really import more of pleasure than pain.

"Ah—ah!" cries Alice, "this is fine, so different to papa's cruel strokes."

"Oh, go on!" says Annie, "you're only just beginning to warm my blood. A little harder will be better now."

Mrs. Sarah is so excited that she furiously rubs her mount and clitoris with her left hand, as she plies the rod with the other.

"Now, Alice!" she cries, "a little harder," as she cuts the firm little bottom into red weals and marks.

Annie now seems lost to what is going on. Her finely developed buttocks heave to each stroke as she rubs her front on the bed, and Alice too seems faint with some curious sensation, as she throws away her birch, rushes to the bed, and rubs her little unfledged mount upon her sister's bottom. Mrs. Sarah continues to use her rod gently, as the girls seem both lost to feeling, so far as her light strokes go.

"Now, my dears, that's only the beginning of the pleasure," cries the housekeeper, as she throws herself on the bed. "Here, Annie dear, come and lie on me, with your belly on my bosom, and open your thighs so that I can kiss your delicious little pussey while you tickle and play with mine. And, Alice, your must kneel beside us, so that my hand can tickle your little slit, while you keep your sister's bottom warm by birching her, but not too hard."

The loving girls, now thoroughly warmed and amorous, eagerly place themselves as desired; Mrs. Sarah greedily seizes upon Annie's charms with her mouth, rolling her tongue in and out the virgin slit and around the small clitoris, just beginning to be developed, between the auburn curls.

"Oh—ah!" cries Annie, "how rude you make me feel, but it's so nice! I can't help nipping your dear face with my thighs; but, oh—oh—Sarah, I must try and give you the same pleasure you give me," she says, as she buries her face in the luxuriant black forest of Mrs. Sarah's cunt, kissing and thrusting in her tongue to the great delight of the housekeeper.

Whisk—whisk—whisk! goes the birch, as Alice exclaims, "Oh, you naughty rude things, to go on so, whilst I am quite forgotten; but my tickler will soon make you know some one else wants a little of the fun."

Each cut make's Annie's bottom twist and wriggle on Mrs. Sarah's face.

"Dear Alice," says the housekeeper, "I did indeed forget you for the moment, but pay us out well. There! how do you like that?" inserting her middle finger as far as it would go in the little virgin slit, which is already moist with excitement.

"I'm not to be so easily satisfied," said Alice.

"I'll pay you out!" Whisk, whisk, goes the birch, as it falls sharply on her sister's bottom, causing her to dance and wriggle with mingled pain and pleasure.

Just at this moment both Mrs. Sarah and Annie are seized with a furious desire as if to eat or bite each other's cunts, and both are lost in the extasy of the moment of spending.

Little Alice at the same time is thoroughly excited by the lascivious working of the finger in her little innocent cunny. "Oh—oh—ah—urr—r," she cries, "it's come upon me too! I feel as if I should faint with delight," as she sinks down by their side on the bed.

Mrs. Sarah now disengages herself from the languid Annie, and throws herself over the younger girl, kissing and tonguing her little slit for her, and at the same time pressing her own longing cunt to the little girl's mouth.

Alice quickly and amorously responds to this attack, whilst the now recovered Annie seizes the birch which her sister had dropped, and applies it vigorously to the housekeeper's already well flayed bum.

"You—you—rude hussies!" she cries, "I'll teach you decency. Sucking each other's things in that way, indeed!"

She seems seized with a fury of disappointed lust, her eyes sparkle, and she grinds her teeth with rage, as she redoubles the force of her blows.

"There—there—there! Ah, you don't mind," she cries. "You dirty things, to go on so!" as she sees them devouring each other's charms with hot kisses and lascivious tongues; but the birch only increases the heat of their desire, till Mrs. Sarah and Alice are both exhausted by a copious spend.

After a little time to recover, the housekeeper says, "My dears, we must not do any more tonight or we may injure your health, but next week, when your father is away, we will have a grand evening with cousin Catherine, and I will show you some funny things I have got to increase our pleasure. Now," she added, "give me a kiss, and say you will love me."

"Yes, yes, we will indeed! you've given us such pleasure!" they both exclaimed.

IV

THE same day that Mr. Warren left home on his business trip witnessed the arrival at his house at Highgate of a fine girl of seventeen, the eagerly expected cousin Catherine, a beautiful blonde with light golden hair, large blue eyes, rather dark arching eyebrows and tall and well-developed figure, promising a rich sight of beauty when unveiled for flagellation.

While sister Alice accompanied her cousin to her room, a serious consultation was held between Mrs. Sarah and Annie respecting the new arrival.

"My dear," said the housekeeper, "she's a fine high-spirited strong girl, it will be a rare treat to see her stripped and prepared for the rod, but how are we to find a cause for chastisement?"

"We must wait a day or two till she is fairly at home," says Annie, "then perhaps we may be able to accuse her of something; she is to sleep with Alice, and I think I can put her up to some device."

"Well Annie, I'm sure you two ought to be as interested as I am in getting her into some scrape," says Mrs. Sarah. "To see a strong, beautiful, and angry girl submit to the birch, is the finest thing in the world."

"But let us wait, and seem to act with stern justice," replies Annie.

"By all means first, but behave as she may we shall give her a taste of the birch before she goes," says the housekeeper.

Nothing occurs for several days, till one morning at luncheon time cousin Catherine does not answer to the summons.

"Where can she be? run and look in the garden, Alice," cries Mrs. Sarah.

Presently the young girl returns, in breathless haste.

"Oh, make haste!" she cries, "come and look! There's Catherine and Maria, the housemaid, standing kissing one another, and looking at the rabbits; they've put the old buck in with the doe, and seem quite to forget everything and what they are doing, as they watch him riding on her back and tumbling off every now and then."

"Now's our time!" cries the housekeeper, "and by good luck, Maria will make another victim."

Saying this she runs out, followed by the two sisters.

The cousin and the servant are so absorbed by the curious emotions they feel at the sight of the lascivious actions of the rabbits, that they are quite unconscious of the approach of the party from the house.

"A fine amusement, indeed, for two rude hoydens," exclaims Mrs. Sarah. "Miss Catherine, and you too, Maria, must be corrected for this."

The startled girls, both blushing crimson, stand speechless before the angry gaze of Mrs. Sarah.

"I—I—I," stammered Catherine, "thought there would be no harm, so I asked Maria to put them together, and they've been fighting ever since."

"Ready to screen yourself with a lie, Miss, eh? Fie, fie!" says the housekeeper, "we must talk this over with you this evening after tea. I don't know if I shan't send you home at once, and discharge Maria. Mr. W— would be horrified at such lewdness."

Luncheon and dinner both pass in gloomy silence. Cousin Catherine has heard of the dreadful birchings Mr. Warren and his housekeeper administer to culprits of the family, and fears she also may taste the smarting rod. Her cheeks alternately turn hot and cold, while the three conspirators secretly enjoy her confusion, and anticipate the coming ceremony.

Eight o'clock finds Mrs. Sarah and two sisters assembled in the drawing room, in full evening dress. The fine large room is brilliantly lighted by numerous wax candles, the centre table has been removed to the further end of the apartment, and the three ladies are seated upon an ottoman which has been put in its place as more convenient for business. The pale Grecian features and dark beauty of the housekeeper form a delightful contrast to the more delicate tints of the fair girls on either side of her; their eyes sparkle with animation, and each heaving bosom is set off by a choice bouquet of deliciously scented flowers, the snowy globes just visible under the gossamer net by which they are supposed to be hid, while ravishing little feet, in blue, white, or pink satin shoes, just peep from under their silken skirts. On a side table close at hand, are spread three or four most elegantly made up birch rods, the green twigs of which have been well soaked in brine for a couple of days past.

Catherine and the servant now enter, both with flashing, indignant looks and scarlet cheeks, although their eyes show signs of recent tears.

"Now, Maria," says the housekeeper, "in Mr. Warren's absence I am the head of the house, and I have resolved to give you a serious whipping for your indecent behaviour with the rabbits this morning. Miss Catherine will have the pleasure of witnessing your punishment before we take her in hand.

"Indeed ma'am, I won't be whipped!" cries Maria, (a stout buxom girl of sixteen, with brown hair and eyes, and ruddy cheeks, who stood looking the very picture of a servant, with her neat, plain dress and small white cap and apron), "especially as I know you want do it on my bare bottom."

"What! you impudent hussey, you refuse, do you? but come Annie and Alice, put her in position, and turn up her clothes to her waist; open her drawers if she has any on, and I will soon let her know what is good for her," exclaimed Mrs. Sarah. "Why if your poor mother only knew she'd slap your bottom herself."

The housekeeper rises to arm herself with a birch, while the sisters attempt to force Maria to the ottoman. Their efforts, how-ever, are in vain, she is too strong.

"Now, Catherine, help your cousins with that donkey of a girl," exclaims Mrs. Sarah.

Strange to say, the strong cousin lends a ready hand. The idea of seeing poor Maria's bum well whipped has a most fascinating effect upon her, and she also hopes to get off lightly herself, by turning on her companion.

"You shall tear the clothes of my back first," cries Maria, as she struggles desperately to avoid the ottoman.

"You bad girl," says Mrs. Sarah, "if you make a noise I'll discharge you without a character."

"Oh—oh—oh, pray, ma'am, do forgive me!" cries poor Maria, the tears running down her cheeks. "It—t—it, was Miss Catherine who wanted to see the rabbits together."

"Oh, you false wretch!" cries Catherine in a rage, " 'twas you told me how funny they would act together, like husband and wife." Saying this she furiously pushed Maria's face downwards on the soft ottoman, and raising her clothes, gave a tremendous slap on the victim's great fat bottom, but which was yet covered with something, for the poor girl not wearing drawers, had secured a large towel over her buttocks, and firmly fastened it in front between her legs.

"Off, off, with that rag, nothing shall cheat us of a bare bum now!" cries the housekeeper.

The victim squeezes her legs tightly together, till Annie and Alice each seize an ancle, and the cousin at once thrusts her hand from behind till she reaches and unties the knot in front.

"There, there, she is ma'am," cries Catherine, as the poor girl's white flesh is exposed, saying which, she pulls up the chemise and skirts well above the waist.

"Now, you troublesome girl, we've got you ready at last," says the housekeeper. "You, Catherine, keep her shoulders down, while the others keep her legs well stretched apart."

"Mercy, mercy! it's a shame to expose me so! oh, oh! do let me off this time, Mrs. Sarah," cries the poor girl.

"No, no, it's for you good, and all bad bottoms must be exposed to the rod," cries the housekeeper, "but I hope the lesson won't be lost on you."

Whisk, whisk, whisk! goes the switch in little strokes at first; whisk, whisk, whisk! they come again a little harder, the flesh beginning to be more rosy at each stroke.

"This is how such rudeness is whipped out of girls like you," cries Mrs. Sarah, giving a smarter cut, which raises deep red marks across her swelling buttocks.

"Oh, oh, ah—a—I can't stand it, dear lady. Do forgive me now," cries the victim.

"You see, Catherine, what you've got to expect when your turn comes. But we haven't half done with this young slut yet—there—there," cries the now furious looking woman, each cut bringing up the weals and marks on the tender flesh.

"My God! oh—ah, I shall faint!" screams the poor girl, "Oh, Miss Annie, save me!"

Mrs. Sarah looks grand in her rage, a very Juno, with her flashing eyes and heaving bust. The left hand holding up the front of her dress so as not to impede her motions, display the splendid shape of leg and ancle encased in flesh coloured silk, and a foot of faultless shape in a blue satin shoe.

Whack, whack, descends the birch in crushing blows, but the poor victim seems almost lost to feeling, when suddenly she receives the clever undercut between her extended thighs, and the lips of her private recess receive a stinging smart.

"Ah—ah—ah, how cruel! you're cutting me to pieces; oh, mercy—mercy! I shall die!" cries poor Maria, as her bottom springs with agony.

"I thought that would keep you from fainting," shouts the housekeeper, as she furiously cuts again and again at the same parts. "To think of a girl, with the hair only just coming on her pussey, to be so forward and rude! I should like to know what you mean by the rabbits doing like husband and wife?"

"Oh—oh—oh, I feel so hot, ah—ah, I can't help it!" exclaimed the victim, suddenly going off into a curious kind of faint, and seeming again lost to feeling, but still wriggling her bottom up and down to each stroke of the now worn out rod.

Throwing the old stump aside, Mrs. Sarah takes a lighter bunch of the green birch, but she seems to gradually grow softer and slower with her strokes as she allows her fury to subside.

The poor bleeding surface of the girl's bottom seems at last to excite Alice's pity, it so dreadfully cut up, and she looks appealingly to he housekeeper.

"My dear Mrs. Sarah," she pleads, "let the poor thing go now; I think she'll be better in future if you don't discharge her."

"Well, then, take her away to bed, my dears, and make haste back; we've got a little more to do, you know," is the reply.

As the two sisters retire with the poor girl Mrs. Sarah goes to a decanter on the side-board, and pouring out some glasses of wine, says, "Come, Catherine dear, we must take a glass to refresh us, it will give you courage to bear your punishment."

"Oh, my dear madam," cries Catherine, throwing herself upon her knees before the housekeeper, "do, do, forgive me now! I'll never do so again, and my parents would be shocked to know I was whipped on my bare bottom."

"No, you must be punished," says the housekeeper, it is for you good. Besides, if you don't submit to be chastised by me, I shall send you home to your father in the morning with a letter explaining your dirty conduct."

"Anything but that," cries the girl.

"Here are your cousins. Now take the wine, then kiss this rod and tell me you deserved it," says Mrs. Sarah.

She drinks, then placing the extended rod to her lips, shudders as she says, "My dear madam, I know I deserve correction, but don't be too hard, you shall find me so good in future."

"Now, Annie and Alice, get her ready at once. It is getting late. Everything off, you know," says the housekeeper.

"No, no, not everything. I can't be so exposed!" cries the blushing girl, "it's too bad."

But the sisters have already unfastened her dress, the skirt falls down to her heels, and almost before she can think what to do, the bodice is removed, and she stands in her stays and petticoats.

"I won't indeed!" she cries, as she pushes Annie aside; "you shan't see me naked."

"Come, come, miss," cries the housekeeper, "it will be worse for you if you resist."

"Oh, spare me, dear madam, a little! you promised not to be too hard," cries Catherine.

"Nothing of the sort, Miss Catherine. I order you to be stripped to your shoes and stockings," said the housekeeper.

The stays undone and three petticoats removed, the shape of her beautiful form begins to be seen, then the finely worked drawers are slipped down, but she clings to her chemise.

Annie, in a fury of desire to behold the fine figure of her cousin, tears the linen from top to bottom. "There, miss," she cries, "we have you at last, for all your obstinacy." And the poor trembling girl's figure is fully exposed.

Her knees touch the ground, but her body is extended on the ottoman as each sister firmly holds one arm.

"There, my dear, that's fine. You can say your prayers as I apply the rod," cries Mrs. Sarah.

"I'll begin gently," she resumes, just whisking the beautiful bottom before her with the tips of the birch.

"Hold, hold!" said Annie, "you know how she slapped Maria. "There!" Spank—spank—spank, went her hand on the lovely posteriors.

"The thought of it make your bottom blush, my dear Catherine."

"Oh—ah! don't, Annie, it's so hard, you hurt so. Wait till I have a chance at you," says her cousin.

"Perhaps you like the birch better dear," said Mrs. Sarah, giving two or three slight strokes.

"Oh, that's not so bad, I rather like it," cries the girl.

"Now for business; bad girls must be whipped, no more play," says the housekeeper, giving a little sharper cut. "There—there— will you want to see the rude rabbits again?"

Each cut raised a redder tint on the fair bum, but the victim did not wince.

"Now, miss, are you sorry for the dirty lascivious ideas you tried to teach my girl Maria?" said Mrs. Sarah.

"Oh—oh—oh, ma'am, I can't stand it, you'll kill me. Oh, be merciful!" cries the girl.

"The birch doesn't kill, it does good," replies the flagellant, increasing the severity of her blows; whisk—whisk—whack—goes the rod, raising great red lines on the skin.

Catherine screams with agony, and writhes in the grasp of the sisters, who hold her firm.

"You bad girl, you can't carry on your games in our house, I can assure you," cries Mrs. Sarah.

"You wicked thing, I suppose you would have begun with your cousins next, but I'll cure you."

"Mercy, mercy!" cries the wretched victim, "it was quite by accident we saw the rabbits."

"Yes, yes," cries Mrs. Sarah, "the cocks and the hens, worms, ducks, geese, pigs, horses, sheep, rats and mice, and rabbits, they all do it, what you call fighting—but I think it will be some time before you study nature again, miss."

Mrs. Sarah now exchanges the worn stump for a beautiful light new birch, and as poor Catherine writhes in her agony, the tender under surfaces come in for stinging cuts, causing intense pain, followed by a glowing heat, in those sensitive parts. She unconsciously wriggles and rubs herself on the edge of the ottoman, each stinging little cut now causing an almost pleasant, rather than painful sensation.

The housekeeper again applies the rod to the already wealed and raw looking buttocks, soon bringing the poor victim to a sense of her situation.

"Now, Miss Catherine, I think this will be a lesson you won't forget in a hurry," she cries, "and I shall soon let you off now."

The poor girl turns her tearful face upon her merciless flagellator, as she exclaims, "Oh, Mrs. Sarah, you have cut my poor bottom almost to ribbons, but just now such a delightful feeling came over me, I seemed in heaven till your cruel strokes woke me up again."

At a sign from the housekeeper, the two girls loose their hold, giving their cousin a kiss at the same time.

"It's all over now, dearie," says Annie, putting the torn chemise over Catherine's head, and at the same time slyly feeling her cousin's hot and moistened virgin gap, as she pretends to pull it down and arrange her drawers; a proceeding which seems highly pleasing to the excited girl, who now throws herself into Mrs. Sarah's arms, and begs her forgiveness for all the trouble she has caused.

"My dears," says the housekeeper, "I will now leave your cousin to your kind care." Don't forget the warm fomentation, then she will be almost well in the morning."

Annie and Alice joyfully lead their cousin to their own room, where she is laid upon the bed and carefully attended to. The elder sister undresses and lies by the side of the suffering girl, while Alice, softly applies the sponge to the poor flayed bum and in between her thighs.

The lights are soon put out, and all three under the sheets, when Annie, nestling close to her cousin, and drawing up her night dress, says, "there, dear, lay yourself on me, it's so comforting to feel each other's flesh; and, oh! Catherine," she whispers, "what a nice little lot of hair you have got, although it is so light coloured we hardly noticed it before. You've more than I have. Feel, dearie?"

Their hands mutually press and caress each other's charms, lips meet in amorous embrace, while soft sighs disturb the silence of the night.

"Ah! ah!" exclaims Catherine, "you two dear girls have indeed made me revel in such pleasure as I never felt before!"

And thus time flies, till all sink into sweet oblivion, dreaming over again the delights they have experienced.

V

"MY dear girls," said the housekeeper, one morning as she sat at breakfast with the two sisters and their cousin, "you know this evening is our last birching soiree before Mr. W— returns from Liverpool, and I think I can promise you an extra treat. I've discovered another fine culprit. What do you think of our fat cook? She's a thief."

"Oh! glorious," cries Catherine, "you shall be the magistrate, let's make up a court, and summarily convict her. Maria can be witness, my cousins two policemen, and I'll be clerk to your worship."

"That will be fine," exclaim both Annie and Alice, "let's serve a summons on her to appear at eight o'clock in the drawing room."

"It shall be done properly, my dears, and as soon as we are dressed we will all go to the costumiers in Bow Street, and order our male attire to be sent up at once. From there we will go to our florist for a good supply of fresh made up rods, nice green ones, better budded than the last he sent us," said Mrs. Sarah.

The day is passed in preparation and delightful anticipation, until nearly eight o'clock, when two very youthful looking policemen suddenly enter the kitchen where fat Mary is sitting ready to faint with fear.

"Is your name Mary Frizzle?" says X 110, laying his hand on her shoulder.

"Yes—sir, but what's the matter?" says Mary.

"You'll soon know when we take you before his worship. Smith, search that dress hanging behind the door, and look round for anything wrong," says 110.

"All right," replies the other officer, proceeding to examine the dress, "why here's a silver tea spoon in the pocket!"

"Miss Frizzle," says No. 110, "I think you're in a bad way, considering the cold meat and fat you've sold at the rag shop."

"Oh, mercy! mercy! what shall I do?" cries Mary, "it's all through my love for my cousin in the guards. Poor fellow, it was only to find him in baccy."

"Soldiers are all rogues, imposing on poor innocent servants," says 110, "why couldn't you take up with a respectable member of the force? Such things never happens then. But come along, I'm sorry to do my duty, and only wish I could run your fine soldier in."

Upstairs to the drawing room the prisoner is marched between the two smart young bobbies, whose tight fitting uniforms display a most unmanly development about the buttocks.

Nearly all the furniture has been cleared away and his worship (Mrs. Sarah) is sitting at a desk fetched from the library, whilst the clerk (Miss Catherine) sits biting a quill at a little table in front.

"Bring the prisoner forward," says the clerk, motioning to a space in front of the table.

"Prisoner, we have no dock, so you must stand there."

"Now, policeman," continues the clerk, "state your charge."

"May it please your worship," says No. 110, "this woman is charged with embezzling provisions, and stealing a silver spoon belonging to Mr. Warren, who is out of town, and your worship, it's all owing to loose morals, and taking up with soldiers."

"Confine yourself to the evidence. You're only a young member of the force, or I should speak sharply," says his worship (Sir Thomas Henry Birch), pulling his whiskers meditatively.

"Yes, Sir Thomas," says 110, "I was a saying as how Mr. Warren is out of town and the housekeeper sent for us to take the charge."

"Go on, my man," says his worship.

"Yes, Sir Thomas, we've been to Bone's rag shop in Cuntfield Lane, a little way up the road and found nearly the whole of a cooked leg of mutton. Mrs. Bones said she bought it of the prisoner last night, besides continual lots of dripping," said 110.

"Stand down for the present," says the clerk, "and let Mrs. Bones get into the box. I suppose she's here, of course."

Mrs. Bones is here sworn on the Worship of Priapus (Maria dressed in character), and turning, makes a low curtsey to his worship.

"Well, woman," says Sir Thomas, "what have you bought of the prisoner?"

"Please, your honour," says Mrs. Bones, "I've known Mary a long time, her and her soldier sweetheart often has a private room in our house on Sundays."

"Oh, you liar!" exclaims the prisoner.

"Silence, prisoner!" says Sir Thomas. "Let the woman go on with her evidence; the police shall enquire into the character of her house."

"Mine's a respectable house, your honour," cries Mrs. Bones. "We only accommodates our servant customers and their gentlemen; we don't admit flaghoppers, no indeed! not in my house!"

"Never mind about your house now," says the clerk. "When did you buy the mutton of her?"

"Last night, your honour. Here it is," says Mrs. Bones, producing the joint in a greasy piece of paper.

"How much did you give for it?" asks the clerk.

"Four pence a pound, and a good price too," says the rag shop keeper.

Police constable Smith, No. 88 X. is now called and sworn. (This is Alice in uniform).

CLERK.—What did you find when the prisoner was taken in charge?

No. 88.—Only this silver tea-spoon in the pocket of her dress (produces spoon, marked J.W.)

CLERK.—Did prisoner make any observation?

No. 88—Yes. That it was all her love for her cousin in the guards.

SIR THOMAS.—Is the housekeeper here?

No. 110.—No, your worship, she is too ill to come to-day, but if a remand—

"Stop!" says Sir Thomas. "Prisoner, you've heard all the evidence; will you plead guilty!"

MARY (whose face has flushed scarlet, and her eyes darting defiant glances of indignation).—Yer worship, them's my perkisites.

"Do you call a leg of mutton your perquisite?" asks Sir Thomas.

"Yer worship, that's an oversight, but indeed it ud been spoilt, as we had a fillet of veal today," pleads Mary.

"That's no reason it should be stolen," says Sir Thomas.

"But it got in along with the fat, my lord," pleads the prisoner.

"Will you plead guilty, and be punished by me or go to another court?" asks the magistrate.

"Oh, no! I never stole any thing in my life," is the answer.

"It will be all the worse for you, if you're so obstinate," says Sir Thomas, "you'll lose both your place and your character."

"Oh, oh! what shall I do? Forgive me, ma'am! Sir Thomas I mean, I didn't think you'd be so severe," cries Mary, sinking on her knees.

"There's no help for it, if you won't plead guilty," says the magistrate, "you must go for trial."

The tears now rolled down the victim's face, as she appealed in vain for mercy. "Ah! Sir Thomas," she cries at last, "if you must punish me yourself, only be merciful, it's my first offence."

"Then," says Sir Thomas, "the sentence is that you be at once well chastised on your bare bottom, till I think you have had enough."

She is at once seized by the two constables (Annie and Alice), assisted by the witness (Maria) and led towards an apparatus which looks like an ordinary pair of steps, minus the staves.

"Oh! my God!" cries the victim, as she spies the rings for tying up her arms and legs, "I won't be fastened to that horrible thing." (It was in fact a Berkeley horse.)

"Never mind her screeching, do your duty," says Sir Thomas, who is getting some fine birch rods out of a drawer.

The trio have already removed the cotton dress, but the woman struggles angrily, as they try to remove her stays; her red face, great heaving bosom, and flashing eyes show the indignation of her soul.

But all in vain. She knows her real guilt, and is afraid to set them at defiance. She may lose both place and character.

Slowly her garments are removed, her wrists secured to the upper rings of the horse, and her ancles to the lower, making a regular spread eagle, as sailors call it.

Now Mrs. Bones (Maria) tears off her shift and leaves the defenceless victim a naked study for their wanton gaze. But such a fat Venus!

Great hanging bubbies fall towards her bloated belly, whilst her buttocks and thighs are perfect lumps of great fat flesh.

Modest white stockings cover her huge calves, in front she is adorned with a perfect forest of reddish brown hair, almost up to her navel, and so long as to reach half down the fat thighs.

"At last, Miss Frizzle," says Sir Thomas, advancing birch in hand, "your immoral and dishonest practices meet their deserts."

"Oh, oh! I'm dead already with fright," screams poor Mary.

"Pooh, pooh the rod will revive you!" exclaims Sir Thomas. "It will do you good—there—there—" just lightly whisking the skin of her bottom.

"Now, will you steal again, Miss Frizzle?" says the operator, cutting rather harder, so as to sting the flesh so distended with fat.

"Ah, ah—ah, you cut so I can't bear it!" cries Mary.

"You call out before you're hurt," answers Sir Thomas. "That's more like a cut!" as whisk—whisk—whack—the birch descends in real earnest, raising the red marks across her buttocks, and making all the surface turn red as if it blushed for shame.

"Now you begin to find out the wickedness of your ways, do

you?" he continued, giving a smart stroke so as to touch the tender parts between her thighs.

The victim struggles to get free, screaming with the intense pain, but to no purpose, She is too securely fixed, and her fat bottom too good a target for the furious flagellant who wields the rod.

"Ah! you feel it, do you?" cries Sir Thomas, growing furious each stroke, harder as it falls, raising great blood marked weals, and long screeches of agony from poor Mary.

"Mercy, mercy! I'll never touch anything again, or even speak to a soldier," she cries.

Sir Thomas's active motions with the rod so disarrange his costume that his wig gets all away, one whisker is lost, and dishevelled locks of coal black hair hang down his back, while the frilled shirt front barely hides two palpitating globes of snowy whiteness, and expose the woman in disguise.

"My God, 'tis mistress! oh, I feared as much!" cried the poor woman, venturing to glance over her shoulder.

"Yes—yes—yes!" cries Mrs. Sarah. "It is indeed me, you wretched thief!" each word bringing down such cuts, that the birch flies in every direction, leaving a wreck of raw mangled flesh all over the writhing buttocks.

"Quick! hand me another!" she cries, throwing aside the worn stump. "Mary Frizzle shall have such a lesson as will make her virtuous and honest in future."

The fresh rod is not quite so heavy as the first, but the strokes are more scientifically delivered; first round the victim's hips almost to reach the hairy forest in front, then cutting the inner surfaces of her thighs, not sparing the great red gaping lips of her Venus's wrinkle.

The agony is greatly increased by the slowness of the strokes, the interval between each blow being intensely painful, in expectation of the stinging cuts.

Poor Mary's cries seem exhausted, and nothing but sobs and groans now accompany the whisking, whacking sound of the rod.

Mrs. Sarah now gradually relaxes in her furious onslaught, and looking round for the spectators, observes that No. 110 and the clerk have each a hand in the other's breeches, while loving tongues dart from mouth to mouth in amorous excitement and close embrace. Policeman Smith is also making love to Mrs. Bones.

To spoil their game, she drops the rod. "There! that's enough! now see her to her bed, and Mrs. Bones shall answer for her share of the business," exclaims the housekeeper.

Poor Mary, now unloosed, presents a sorry spectacle of mangled flesh from her loins almost to her knees, great beads of perspiration stand upon her face, as they hastily throw her skirts over her and lead her away groaning.

"Mrs. Bones," says the housekeeper, as her assistants return, "you are to be blindfolded, while we four will each have a bunch of twigs to quicken your motions with, till you catch one of us."

"Yes, yes, we won't hurt you!" exclaim the others catching hold of her.

"No, no, no, I won't!" screams Maria, struggling to free herself.

"Don't waste time, my dear. Off with her clothes, the more trouble she gives the harder we'll hit," says the housekeeper.

Resistance is quite hopeless. First the rag-shop keeper's wig is pulled off, the coarse stuff gown follows; stays and petticoats offer but a faint obstacle, and while one ties the bandage firmly across her eyes, the others tear off her shift; then each giving a good smack on her firm arse with their hands, she is left to probe for her tormentors, who each speedily arm themselves with a light switch of birch.

Maria's face is flushed with anger, but her fine compact figure is a study for an artist. Her loose dark brown hair hangs over a pair of beautifully moulded white shoulders that any lady might be proud of; a firm and fleshy back and rounded buttocks complete the view behind, while in front her small well rounded bubbies bewitch the gaze. Add to these attractions, a ravishing waist, slightly high stomach, and finally, the mount of love, just beginning to be fledged with soft brown curls, which her hands vainly strive to hide; further down, the swelling thighs and finely shaped legs terminate in neat ancles and boots.

"You must make better use than that of your hands, Miss Modesty," cries Catherine, giving her bottom a smart little switch.

"Ah!" cries Maria in a rage, "it's a shame to serve me so, but I'll soon catch some one."

"This way, then," says Mrs. Sarah, giving another sly cut between the poor girl's legs.

"You wretches!" cries the furious Maria, "I'll birch the first I catch."

"Here I am," says Alice, stooping down and giving an un-expected pull at the little brown curls between her legs.

"Now I've got some one!" cries Maria, as she fancies herself safe, but stumbles forward on the floor.

"Ha! ah!! ah!!! Miss Clever!" they cry, "get up and try again." With this they shower a storm of light blows on her devoted bum, bringing a red blush all over the surface. She is soon up again, rushing up and down the room in her frantic desire to catch one of her enemies, but getting well paid out for her trouble as they easily evade her clutches.

At last, almost exhausted and mad with rage, she falls again; but while they are eagerly using their rods upon her devoted bottom, she manages to slightly shift the bandage, so as to see a little with one eye.

Her smarting bum adds fresh strength to her desire for vengeance; watching her opportunity, she pins Miss Catherine in a corner, and regardless of the blows of the others, secures her prize.

"Now," cries Maria, "my fine gentleman, I'll soon have your breeches down to your heels!"

Assisted by the others, the struggling cousin's garments are speedily unbuttoned, and her fine buttocks exposed to slaps and cuts, her captor holding her across her lap.

Now they strip and blindfold her as quickly as possible, and Maria starts her off on her chase with a stinging slap of her arse.

She is very cautious at first, but the stinging cuts of the rods make her more active in a very short time.

Again and again she tries to secure a victim, and presently Mrs. Sarah gives her a smart cut right between her thighs.

"Ah, ah!" cries Catherine, "that's Maria; she wants to serve me out; but mind I don't catch her."

"Now she's down," they shout, as the indignant girl stumbles over a hassock, their rapid blows making her bottom one mass of red, and even slightly drawing the blood, so infuriated and merciless do they become with their heated blood; but with a sudden and unexpected swoop of her arms Catherine pulls down all four upon her, exclaiming, "There! you're fairly caught. I've got the lot at once."

"We're all too tired to struggle," says Mrs. Sarah, "and it's getting late, so Catherine, forego your spite against us, and another time you shall start the revels as you please. My dears," she continued, "I promised to show you some little instruments of pleasure, but it must be deferred till another time. We will say good night, now.

END OF VOL. I.

CURIOSITIES

OF

FLAGELLATION,

A SERIES OF INCIDENTS,

And Facts Collected by an Amateur Flagellant.

Volume II.

MRS. NORTH'S SCHOOL.

BIRCHGROVE PRESS,
MMXV.

THE CURIOSITIES OF FLAGELLATION.

I.

Letter from Sir Charles Wildish to Mrs. North.

Dear Madam,

You some time since expressed a wish to know how I manage to gratify my penchant for flagellation of young girls, when I do not visit your establishment.

I may observe that my modus operandi is simplicity itself; human nature is so venal that money will purchase almost any gratification we may desire, and instruments willing to pander to our lascivious ideas are always readily found.

Just now I have in my pay a lady who keeps a first class seminary for the daughters of the aristocracy, clergy, or professions (at least so her prospectus runs), the children of tradespeople being rigorously excluded, terms for each pupil one hundred guineas per annum, &c., &c.

She occupies a fine large house, situated at Fulham, standing in extensive grounds, surrounded by a high wall on every side. The scholars number at least fifty or sixty, besides, English, French, German, and Italian governesses; a fine field you must admit for the exercise of our gentle craft, as old Isaac Walton would say.

The head of this establishment happens to be an old flame of mine, whom I seduced some twenty years since, when she was only about seventeen, and a most accomplished lady I have found her ever since, as she is really talented, and brings on her pupils famously (owing, I believe, in a great measure, to her known unflinching severity); besides she is so clever in expedients to gratify me (her partner in the business, my share of which is worth at least a thousand a year); thus you see I have managed to combine pleasure with profit and only require to visit your world-renowned hostelrie, when I want a little variety in my erotic vagaries.

Miss Whippington is now a fine specimen of a fat, fair, and forty style of beauty, with a finely formed commanding figure, blue eyes, and light flaxen hair, with a leg which when cased in her flesh-coloured stockings equals anything ever shown by the famous Madame Vestris, and I may here remark that I have a peculiar letch for silk stockings and handsome boots on the ladies I see, in fact were they not attired to my satisfaction in that way I should turn with loathing from the most delightful woman in the world, and my bedfellows have to keep them on all night, for fear I might see their naked legs at any time.

In our select academy Friday afternoons are sacred to St. Bridget, but sometimes specially bad conduct requires almost instant punishment, in which case a message is immediately sent to my house, which is not far distant.

You will be greatly surprised to hear that the place for carrying out the infliction of punishment is on the ground floor, and more so still when I tell you that the conservatory is used for that purpose, a luxuriously furnished little room, opening by folding glass doors into the same, is my hiding place, and enables me to ensconce myself free from observation behind the foliage of some fine plants, expressly placed so as to hide my corner, where I have both a chair and footstool placed so as to be at my ease during thrilling exhibitions; there is no risk of discovery as all present attend like soldiers on parade drill, not being allowed to ramble about, and are marched off all together at the conclusion of the ceremony.

I think you will agree with me that this is a truly refined arrangement, as flowers have such a voluptuous effect on our senses, and add to the pleasure of the scene, which far exceeds anything you can produce for your patrons, with your hired assistants; the knowledge that the pretty culprits are bona fide victims gives me an excess of erotic pleasure I cannot properly describe.

Last Friday I attended in my place, as M.Ps are wont to say, but before the business commences I will just observe that the space set apart for the purpose, is a considerable distance, quite forty yards from the entrance door, communicating with the house, which is always securely locked as soon as the party have passed through, so as to preclude all chance of interruption. The arrangements are very simple, a space some twenty feet by thirty, is neatly paved with various coloured encaustic tiles, laid in an elegant design, and a fountain with artificial work adorns the oblong square is a perfect forest of tropical plants, and choicest flowering shrubs, the warm atmosphere produced by artificial heat, making indeed a paradise of the place for our purpose. The only furniture consists of a comfortable armchair, placed in the middle facing the fountain, with a small table in front covered with a crimson cloth, on which lay a book with pens and inktstand, besides several neatly tied rods of newly cut birch twigs, of which we have a profusion growing in various parts of the grounds.

Now I am settled in my ambuscade, and Miss Whippington makes her appearance, accompanied by Mdlles. Valerie and Ripperi, and Frau Steinbach, the French, Italian and German governesses, there are also three young ladies, evidently the misdemeanants from their agitated looks.

"Lady Flora Bumby," says Miss W., seating herself in the chair and opening the book, "stand forward Miss, and attend to what I have to say."

Lady Flora, a slightly made, meek looking, fair girl, of about fourteen, with large light blue eyes full of tears, comes tremblingly up to the table, her quivering lips seeming unable to utter a word in her distress.

"So my lady," continues Miss W., "it has come to this, has it?" looking at the book and reading, "Monday, imperfect French lesson; Tuesday, great inattention in geography; Wednesday, Thursday, and to-day, no improvement, very careless all the week; very fine indeed, as if your papa, the Earl, sent you to my school to idle over your lessons, now you have been so repeatedly admonished and told of the consequences, that it is useless to defer correction any longer; Mdlle. Valerie will administer a light chastisement on your bottom, and I hope the shame and degradation will benefit your studies, or the next time your ladyship comes under the birch you may expect great severity. Steinbach, you, and Mdlle. Ripperi put the naughty girl in proper order, and then horse her on your back."

The German governess, a buxom fine young woman, power-fully built, takes hold of the little lady and, assisted by the Italian, the muslin dress and silk sash are quickly removed.

But now the poor girl, bathed in tears, finds her voice, "Oh! oh! pray, Miss Whippington, do, do, forgive me this time"——

"No, no," cries the schoolmistress, "your promises of amendment are only idle words, perhaps the rod will cure you of making empty promises in future."

The girl's spirit now comes to her assistance, the timid tearful face is changed to one of blushing indignation, as her petticoats are raised and pinned well up above her waist, giving just a glimpse of her fair skin, as seen between the opening of her drawers, next these also are the chemise tucked up as high as possible, fully exposing her delicately rounded buttocks and beautiful white thighs, which as well as her legs are straight and elegant, the extremities being well set off by charming little shoes and silken hose.

Steinbach now takes her up, assisted by Ripperi, the victim's hands go round her neck and are fast held in front, whilst unwittingly her legs cling round the German's waist thus presenting all her backward charms ready for the birch. Mdlle. Valerie is already armed with a nice light bunch of twigs, her sparkling dark eyes plainly showing the pleasure she anticipates.

"Now, Mdlle., proceed," says Miss W., "it will do her good."

The French governess is only too pleased to commence, and a first swift little cut brings the carmine hue upon the tender flesh.

"One, two, three, four," counts Miss W., as each stroke leaves its mark on the devoted little bum; "harder, if you please, Mdlle. you're too tender with her."

"Oh! oh! I can't bear it any longer," screams Lady Flora in agony, as five, six, seven fall in smarting successions, "I will indeed be good—ah—ah."

"Eight, nine, ten!" counts Miss W., as the poor bottom gets redder and shows small weals, "three more good cuts will make a baker's dozen for the lazy, idle girl, she shall have double next time."

Whisk, whisk, whisk, the three last blows cut through the air, and leave the poor girl almost fainting as she is let down with her bottom in a smarting agony.

"I'm sorry to have punished you, but Flora dear, it is for your good, and I hope will not be necessary again; now what has the Honourable Miss Mason done?" looking in the book. "Oh, I see, very disgraceful, quarrelling with Miss Howard and slapping her face—fighting indeed. I'll fight you with a good birch," rising and looking very angry.

"Madam, she insulted me, called me names," exclaimed Miss Mason, a dark girl about sixteen with flashing eyes and burning cheeks.

"No excuse for behaving like a low girl. Miss Howard will have to answer for her conduct presently," said Miss W., selecting a fine heavy rod.

The governesses do not wait for orders, but at once seize their victim, and not heeding her remonstrances, speedily divest the struggling girl of her clothing. Dress, corset, petticoats and drawers are pulled off.

"Oh—oh—not naked," screams the girl, as she clings to her chemise, "it's shameful, disgusting."

"How dare you, Miss, use such language in reference to my orders, let your chemise go at once or it will be torn off, and make it still worse for your wicked bottom," cries Miss W. "Off with it, and make her kneel on the chair."

The chair is properly placed, and Miss Mason made to kneel with her fine plump bottom well presented to the operator, whilst the three governesses hold her down over the back of the chair, and even little Flora seems to forget her own smart as seeing the preparations, whilst Miss Howard seems positively delighted at the scene.

"Now, will you strike any one again, Miss?" cries Miss W., giving a smart cut fully on the tightly bent skin. "If things go on like this, we shall get black eyes in school some day."

Whisk—whisk, goes the rod, as her fury keeps increasing, weals and red marks follow each stroke.

Poor Mason writhes under each smarting cut, exposing every now and then the pouting red lips of her most secret charms, beautifully fringed with jet black hair.

"You quarrelsome minx, this will be a lesson to you," cries Miss W., making the birch fly in all directions by the furious energy of her blows, not even sparing the inner surfaces of her tender thighs and dark mossy grotto of love, making the parts to smart and burn by turns.

The high couraged girl grinds her teeth with agony and indignant rage, but utters no cry, and in a few minutes more seems almost lost to sensation, such a sweet pleasant expression comes over her face as she twists and nips her thighs to-gether.

The schoolmistress also at the same time seems to experience something of the same feelings, as if the birch united her to her victim by some magnetic sympathy, her blows relax, and instead of the furious flagellant, her expression changes to one of languishing love, as she orders the poor girl to be released, saying with tears in her eyes: "It is indeed painful to chastise your beautiful bottom; come, my dear, and kiss me, and say you will be better tempered in future."

Miss Mason seems to quite forget all about her raw looking flayed bum, as she quickly rises and gives her flagellator a rapturous loving kiss, conclusively proving the attractive influence of the birch when wielded by one who throws her soul in the work.

Sitting down in the chair Miss W. regains her stern composure, as the governesses quickly replaces the clothes on the now smiling girl, who stands with sparkling eyes and heaving bosom, which are evident signs of most pleasing emotions, especially when she regards the now anxious face of red-haired Miss Howard.

"You may well look serious, Miss," says the school-mistress, turning towards the last named young lady, "such conduct as yours can only be chastised by my own hands; there, no excuses, I intend to stop once for all, the use of unlady like language in my establishment."

Miss Howard, a short stout red-haired girl of about seventeen, with dark brown eyes, turns pale and blushes by turns, as she passively allows the removal of her dress till suddenly, as the last vestige of covering is taken from her, she throws herself on her knees before Miss W. "Oh, madame, I beg you and Miss Mason a thousand pardons," she cried, sobbing, "I—I—know I must be punished, but do, do, do be merciful, I shall die if you cut me so, indeed I shall!"

"I hate a coward," cried Miss W. "Get upon the chair," giving her a good cut across the loins leaving a fine red impression of the twigs on her fat bottom.

"Ah—ah—ah," roared the girl, rolling over and kicking, regardless of the immodest exposure of all her parts, and showing her fine small firm breasts, the red covering of her mount, and even the lips and opening of her virgin slit, plump round arse, short full thighs, and good legs encased in pink silk stockings.

"Get up, you bad girl," cries Miss W., giving cut after cut across the hips, thighs, and even on the mount, (but not too hard) as the girl continues to writhe and scream.

"Well, then lay there and take your whipping, if you won't get up," cries the schoolmistress, "only turn her on her face, and hold her legs."

"Ah—ah—ah! mercy," screams Miss Howard, as the governesses, Miss Mason, and even little Flora, eagerly help to hold her down.

"Now, you bad mannered girl," says Miss W., as regardless of the screams she cuts and thrashes with all her might. "I almost wish I had expelled you at once, instead of taking this trouble."

"Oh, madame, dear madame," moans the victim, "I'm dying in agony; mercy, mercy—ah," she screams again.

Miss W. soon wears the rod to a useless stump upon the mangled and bleeding bottom of the poor girl, who really faints away between her pain and terror.

"Chère, take her away," says Miss W., sinking exhausted into the chair. "Miss Mason and Lady Flora you had better go to bed, to recover yourselves, Frau Steinbach will see some refreshment sent up to you. Leave me."

I observed Miss Mason put her arms round the little Flora and give her a loving kiss, as they retired with the others.

My pego was bursting with impatience, and I could scarcely wait till assured of all being gone, when my lady love, taking up a birch rod as a signal, I emerged from my concealment, and hastily conducted her to the sofa in the little room I have mentioned.

"You naughty man, now do your duty to me or it will be the worse for you," she exclaimed, reclining on the sofa, and pulling me upon her, her hand instantly unbuttoning and guiding my inflamed priapus to her well moistened and longing cunt. For more than two hours we indulged our most erotic ideas, Miss W. from time to time reviving my drooping energies by a vigorous application of the rod.

She afterwards told me that visiting Lady Flora and Miss Mason in their room, she found the two dear girls fast asleep in each other's embrace, evidently exhausted by mutual pleasure as they lay entwined belly to belly with their hands on each others secret charms.

You must admit, my dear Madame, that such pleasure, combined with business, is a good speculation.

Yours truly,
C. WILDISH.

CHAPTER II.

Sir Charles Wildish to Mrs. North.

Dear Madam,

You press me to send some further account of my experiences as a flagellant. Let me first begin my letter with two or three little anecdotes, and afterwards I will finish with something I have seen myself.

Some few years ago Inspector Golden was a well-known officer of the L division of Metropolitan Police, but unfortunately was so addicted to drink, that for the last few years his position in the force was most precarious, and he was in constant danger of dismissal, until one afternoon he was so drunk as actually to fall from the top of an omnibus just opposite the station, and being severely injured the intoxication was overlooked, and he quietly retired on his pension.

This man used to come home to his house very often the worse for drink, and sometimes quite incapable, when his wife, a fine strapping woman of forty, would get into a violent passion, and having got him on the sofa in their parlour, would turn him on his face, pull down his trousers as far as the knees, and arming herself with a heavy dog whip would lay on his bare posteriors with might and main, regardless of his curses, groans, and threats of what he would do to her.

The castigations were most beneficial in sobering the man, but comparatively useless as a stimulant to venery, the wife being compelled after her exertions in aid of temperance, to solace herself in the arms of my informant, a fine young fellow who lived in the house, who used to prepare himself for the encounter by looking at Mrs. Golden through the keyhole as she whipped her husband.

Lord Coachington who had lived a very fast bachelor life, married at the age of thirty a wealthy young widow some three or four years his junior, of most prepossessing appearance, and every way qualified for the joys of matrimony; to their great mortification however he from the first proved perfectly incapable of doing the husband's part expected from him by her ladyship.

She was no novice in the art of love, and after the first night or two was quite carried away by her lust in endeavours to raise his poor limp affair to a state of action, she sucked, fingered, and played with his pego and balls, in every possible manner, and in her heated, excited state threw herself over his face, pressing her longing, amorous cunt down to his mouth and tongue, spending profusely over his moustache and beard, as she furiously rubbed her mount backwards and forwards, but all in vain.

"My dear, says Lord C., "I'm used up by my early vices, begun whilst at Eton and the rapid dissipation I have indulged in since, but," says the slydog, "I've been reading a book on the use of flagellation in cases of impotency, do let me try it by lightly birching your bottom with the rod, to see if it has any effect on me, I feel almost certain it will, the idea is so novel, and takes my fancy so."

"No, indeed," says her ladyship, "if you can't do without that I must have a divorce."

"My darling," says Lord C., "you distress me by talking so; do love me still, I will give you anything you can wish or think of if you will humour me only this once."

"I won't, I can't," says her ladyship, "I've heard how cruel and furious the birching is, and suspect your lordship is an old hand at the birching science."

"Indeed? I've never touched or felt a birch since I was at school, and then I noticed how stiff my little cock used to get, and how nice and warm I felt down there when not punished severely. But I want to go through the regular form with you that I've have been reading of; you must be properly tied up and secured, with your bottom well exposed, and such a fancy have I taken to see you so, that I feel that the sight of your bottom, looking rosy and warm, would at once effect, our purpose. Do, dearest, consent; say what shall I give you?"

"Well, then, only this once," she says at last, "if you give me a cheque for £ 10,000 to spend on what I please for myself. I must also have a dildoe, and be allowed to birch you in return some day."

"My brave darling," he said, embracing, her, "better than that, I've got two Bank of England notes for £ 5,000 each in my pocket book. I meant to tempt you with one, and then both if necessary. Now you shall have them at once," jumping out of bed.

"There dear," he says, handing them to her eager grasp, as she also gets up. "Ever since I got the Domestic scenes I've been itching to try the birch. See what a nice little one is provided already," showing a light green birch tastefully tied up with blue silk ribbons. "Now, you must first be secured."

Leading her back to the bed, from underneath which he produces a coil of fine silken rope. "Now dear," he says, "stand with your legs wide apart, so. Now lay your belly across the bed with your bottom just over the edge this side." Quickly securing the rope round each ankle, he carries it round the legs of the bedstead, so as to keep her legs well stretched apart, and bringing the two ends together at the other side, secures her hands, so that she is regularly spread eagled, and perfectly helpless, with her night dress rolled up to her armpits.

"Oh! William, my dear," she cries, "how you have exposed me. You'll keep your promise, and not be too hard, won't you?"

"You mercenary woman," says his lordship, "do you think you're to have that lump of money for child's play, no, no, indeed. I'll have my money's worth!" kissing her beautiful white buttocks, and giving them a hearty slap—"there that's for luck."

"You brute, you'll kill me," she cries. "I believe I've married a monster."

"A brute and a monster, eh!" says his lordship, flourishing the birch. "You'll think better of me bye-and-bye."

Whack—whack—whack, go three light strokes.

"My dear," he says, "are you going to spend all that money on yourself?"

"Why not?" says she, "you've got plenty—oh—ah—ah! that's too hard."

"Can't be too hard, for such a greedy woman," he replies, with a sharp cut, just touching her up between the thighs.

"Oh, oh! oh!" she screams, as his sharp strokes descend on her naked bottom. "Ah—r—r, you're cutting me to pieces."

His eyes glisten, and his relentless arm puts more force into every blow as he says, "oh—oh—indeed, not much yet for £ 10,000."

"Let me go," she screams in agony, "and take back your notes. Oh—oh—ah—mercy."

"No, not for double and treble the money now," he exclaims, getting furious, and smashing the twigs in pieces at every stroke.

Her ladyship moans and writhes in speechless agony, till at last her bottom presents a broad expanse of weals and marks, all raw and red.

Her husband has no pity, but his hitherto limp affair now begins to rise and stick out beneath his shirt, and at last, as he perceives his victim subside into a kind of extatic swoon, he throws away the stump of the birch and directing his now tremendously swollen pego at the mark plunges into her hot and well lubricated cunt, where he gives and receives the most voluptuous pleasure.

After the first course she is released and repays upon his devoted arse a double allowance of what she has received from him.

I need not say that he was sincerely forgiven, and that she had the spending of the money, but I must tell you that the application of the birch made them perfectly happy; her ladyship in due time gave birth to twins (two girls, and now they go on so well that the lady's maid has to attend their revels, and birch one or the other of them in their love gambols. Occasionally Lord C. takes a fancy to the pretty maid, but his spouse is so amiable she only vents her jealousy on their bottoms.

I once knew a Mr. Robinson who spent all his fortune to gratify his letch for peculiar kinds of flagellation, and died in a lunatic asylum, when no longer able to indulge his propensity for the birch.

About the age of thirteen he was sent to a fashionable boarding school, kept by a talented young Master of Arts from Cambridge, who soon vitiated such of the pupils, as he found of a suitable temperament, in all the vices of sodomy, frigging, sucking, and flagellation; several nights every week he had a regular orgie in his bedroom with five or six of his favourite boys.

Charley Robinson has often told me that the master's peculiar fancy was generally to have himself tied to the bedstead, and flagellated at once by two or three of the boys with heavy birch rods, whilst one or two others played with his fine cock in every conceivable way of titillation.

You may imagine that such early introduction to the virtues of the rod had a great influence on his erotic pleasure in after life, in fact when he left school at eighteen his constitution was so enervated and debilitated by his debaucheries that he was almost unable to procure an erection without the application of sovereign remedy.

Going to live with an old uncle, who had made him his heir, he soon seduced two fine young maid servants to his purposes, who managed secretly to indulge him with lessons in his bedroom at night, but female society soon pulled upon his taste, and nothing but flagellating or being flagellated by males would answer his end.

The uncle dying in a year or two left him sole master of a large fortune, which for a time he spent with profusion in procuring subjects for his birch; he kept two fine well-formed young pages, as well as two footmen, with whom he indulged his erotic ideas, but his appetite for new male bottoms was so insatiable that if he saw a fine handsome youth in the street, it was a case of love at first sight, and he would lavishly expend any amount of money to accomplish his ends.

One afternoon in Regent Street he made the acquaintance of an aristocratic looking youth, dressed in the height of fashion, and after a few preliminary remarks he succeeded in inducing him to accept of some refreshment at a neighbouring hotel, where Mr. R. so far improved the acquaintance, as to elicit the fact that the young gentleman was rather hard up, through losses on the turf, which he dared not mention to his father.

My friend now hinted that if he would do him a favour the amount he would assist him with would be no object.

"Ah, no," says the youth, "my case is hopeless, how would a stranger lend £ 5000, less would be no use?"

"Look here, boy," says Mr. R., displaying his pocket-book full of notes for a large amount, "would you be grateful if I stood your friend eh?"

"Anything short of life itself my dear sir," says the youth, "but it's simply ridiculous to think you mean it."

Although they were alone, Mr. R. leaned across table and whispered in his ear.

"No, no," says the young gentleman, flushing scarlet, "not for a thousand, nothing but the amount I mentioned would save me from disgrace that or nothing if you really mean it," shedding tears, and holding his handkerchief to his eyes. "Nothing would— would tempt me, but the thought of my mother breaking her heart, when she knows how I have gambled."

"Well," exclaims Mr. R,, "is it a bargain for £ 5000. You shall have the money down as soon as we get to my house in Piccadilly."

"Yes—yes, I suppose I must, but it's so terrible, don't keep me in suspense," says the youth.

Mr. R, leads the way to a cab, his house is speedily reached, and the new victim duly introduced to his four acolytes.

"Thomas," says his master, to one of the footmen, "we want to begin business at once, as time presses. Have all ready without delay."

"Yes, sir," says Thomas, "the study is always ready. I have been doing it up this morning, as I fancied you would bring some one home."

Mr. R. at once conducted his guest to the study, a fine large room, fitted up with book shelves, library fashion, and also decorated with several pictures of various kinds of birch discipline.

A packet of bank notes was at once handed to the young gentleman, who secured them in his breast pocket, and unfastening his trousers bared his backside for the rod, but Mr. Thomas the footman, calling one of the pages to his assistance, proceeded to undress the victim, who strongly remonstrated and endeavoured to avoid further exposure of his person.

My friend Robinson now advancing birch in hand, calls out: "Yes, that's right, no clothes on such a beautiful Adonis."

But Adonis was obdurate. "You shall not strip me," he cries "I didn't bargain for that."

"Never mind his nonsense," cries R. "Here you John and George," addressing the other footman and page, "just lend a hand to strip him."

Resistance is vain, coat and vest are soon removed and they try to take off his breeks, but Thomas suddenly call out; "Good God, sir, he's no cock, I do believe it's a woman."

"Tear the things off," cries R. in a rage; "Damn me if I don't pay her off if it is."

A few moments only and the young gentleman is reduced to a beautiful nude female, blushing and screaming for mercy.

She is soon horsed on John's stout back, and her legs firmly held by the others, who are all in a rage at the imposition.

"Ah! Ha!" cries Robinson, commencing a furious attack with the birch. "I'm not sorry now that you are a girl, it seems to suit my humour. I'll birch you first and my four fellows shall all fuck you well as I birch them afterwards."

No mercy was shown to the poor girl, whose beautiful tender bum was literally cut to pieces, till she fainted from pain and extatic agony combined. She was now laid on a couch and Mrs.

Thomas, John, George and Fred all fucked her well in turn as their backsides were birched to keep up the motion.

The poor girl seemed to gain fresh strength with each encounter, as they only increased her lubricity instead of allaying the venereal furore excited by the flagellation, so much so that she even permitted R. to finish by sodomising her, and when she had worn them all out, "hoped she might be allowed to earn another £ 5000 in the same pleasant way."

Now, for myself, as a conclusion to this long letter, yesterday afternoon I received from Miss Whippington notice of a summary conviction for gross misconduct of one of the girls, and at once hastened to my post in the conservatory. My amiable *chère amie* soon appeared with the culprit, a fair slender looking girl of about thirteen or fourteen, escorted by the three governesses as before.

Seating herself in a chair Miss W. takes a fine bunch of birch off the table, and looking sternly at the fair girl, commences, "Miss Lucy St. Clair, such conduct as yours can only be put down by instant condign punishment; talking over the wall to those rude boys in the next garden, why, the young rascal must have had a ladder to enable him to look over and this letter found in your pocket reads:—

"Dear Lucy, I send you lots of kisses, won't we have a hug when we meet in the lane tomorrow, at half-past six.—Signed, Charlie.

"Pray, miss, who is Charlie, and how should he know your name? Fine goings on for a respectable boarding-school, we shall have the young ladies going home with the dropsy next, or something very much like it."

"I won't go near the wall again, if you forgive me madam," whimpered the abashed girl, "indeed I never encouraged the boy."

"You're only making the case worse by gratuitous lies," exclaims Miss W., "make haste and prepare her for the rod."

Poor Lucy finds no sympathy from the eager governesses, who commence at once to disrobe their victim.

She is slender, as I said before, but as her charms are gradually unveiled by the ruthless hands of her tormentors she at last stands a picture of grace and symmetry, her spirituelle expression of face harmonises so perfectly with the fairy development of her figure, and modesty herself could not have been better personified as the blushing girl stood holding her hands, where the daughters of Eve always fancy they require a screen of fig leaves or something else.

She is now placed kneeling on the chair, and a strap is passed over her back and underneath the seat to keep her steady, her legs being held by the German and Italian ladies, who, as they kneel slightly below their victim on either side, evidently gloat on the delightful prospect of her most secret beauties; the little rosy lips of her almost unfledged cunny, the rising mount still partially screened by one hand, and, above all, the delicately round, firm, white globes, of her tender bottom.

"Now, Miss St. Clair, this will be something to keep you out of lovemaking for a while," says Miss W., giving a light preliminary whisk on the beautiful little bum.

"Oh! madam, do have mercy," cries poor Lucy.

"Not yet, you must have your deserts," cries Miss W., "one, two, three, four," increasing the strength of the strokes at each word.

The young lady evinces a deal more courage than was to be expected, her poor bottom turns pink, then red, as the marks and weals are more visible, the only evidence of her suffering is in the writhing and flinching of her buttocks, as each smarting blow descends.

"Now, will you encourage, those bad boys again?" cries the schoolmistress, working herself into a fury.

"Ah! madam—do—do—have pity now," screams the girl in her agony.

Whisk—whisk—whack, goes the rod in heavy cuts, drawing faint marks of blood on the bruised surface of the skin, each stroke seems as if it must finish the poor victim; the governesses even look as if appealing for mercy, and at last Miss W. relaxes the force of her blows, as the rod is almost worn away and strewed in fragments over the place.

"There, you bad girl, now kiss me, and ask my pardon, or I will send you home in disgrace," cries Miss W.

Again the magnetic influence of the birch asserts itself, and the poor bruised girl seems to forget her hurts as she throws herself sobbing in the lady's arms, receiving and giving rapturous kisses of forgiveness.

"There, my dear," at last says Miss W., "you'll be good in future, now go to your room and let Frau Steinbach attend to your poor sore little bum."

They all retire, and this pretty little scene had such an exciting effect on my rampant organ, that for a long three hours I experienced the most voluptuous pleasures, in every variety, the amorous Miss W. could suggest.

I strongly suspect it is a case of the wolf and the lamb between her and her pupils, when she has a sudden fancy for my company. I will send you a little more of the ways of the world some day, and remain,

    Yours truly,
        C. WILDISH.

CHAPTER III.

Mrs. North to Sir Charles Wildish.

Dear Sir Charles,

Many thanks for your last letter, and in return for your kindness in taking the trouble to write so much for my edification, I send you a true copy of the diary of one of my most distinguished patrons, no less than the late Lord P., who was a most devoted advocate of birch discipline.

I need not trouble you with any remarks of my own, as you used to know his lordship so well yourself, and merely add that any time you honour me with a visit I will with pleasure show you the original MS.

"My love for the birch was acquired at the early age of nine, when I so well remember my lady mother one day calling me and my two dear sisters into her boudoir, informed us that as we were without the authority of a father to control us we were getting quite too troublesome for her to manage, consequently she had engaged a very talented young lady of the name of Varcoe, who had been highly recommended to her for strict discipline and perseverance with her pupils. "Indeed, my dears," continued our mother, "Miss Helen Varcoe would not accept the responsibility of your education unless I gave her carte blanche to use the birch as she might think necessary, so you will have to mind your P's and Q's, my dears."

I have often thought, as I remembered the dear old lady's words in after years, did P's and Q's refer to pricks and quims; who first originated the expression is a question worthy of discussion.

"Oh! mamma, dear!" exclaimed my sisters in a breath, (they were both much older than myself, one twelve and the other thirteen), "you surely won't allow her to beat us, it may be all very well for boys like Percy, but we're big girls now."

"My dears, indeed she will," replied her ladyship, "it's nothing to what girls in my time had to submit to; when I went to school my poor bottom often smarted under the rod if I did not know my lessons, or other misconduct, and I quite agree with those who think it a most wholesome mode of correction, you are to be entirely under Miss Varcoe, and it will be useless to appeal from her to me as I have every confidence in her discretion."

"What a shame!" we all exclaimed, "perhaps she'll turn out a brute."

"Now, my children," says our mother, "Miss Varcoe will arrive here the day after to-morrow, and I very much mistake if you do not all of you soon taste her birch, unless you make up your minds to be good, you two girls are getting regular tom-boys, and Percy as bad as he can be, it was indeed time to get a good determined lady to look after you."

This was on a Wednesday, and the following Friday at luncheon we were duly introduced to Miss Helen Varcoe, (I have ever since considered that a lucky Friday).

"My dear Miss Varcoe, you will find them sadly behaved I am afraid, I haven't had the courage to check them as I ought, but perhaps they will do better with you."

"I hope so, my lady, they look such nice young ladies, and I am sure his little lordship will be a great favourite of mine," replied our governess, who was a middle sized plump young lady of about three and twenty, with cold regular features and dark eyes, her eyebrows being particularly black and bushy, as well as the darkly defined moustache on her upper lip, which gave a most masculine appearance to her face, but in speaking she showed such a lovely set of pearly teeth, and had such a pleasant dimple on her cheeks that we seemed both awed and fascinated at the same time.

Castle Romney, the fine country mansion to which we had retired ever since my poor father's death, was built in the Elizabethan style, a fine imposing front with wings on either side, and my mother had prepared quite a suite of apartments for us and our new governess in the left wing over the blue drawing room, so that the servants' offices being all situated in the opposite wing of the building, we were well away from general observation.

The study or schoolroom was at the further end of the corridor which ran the whole length of the wing, so that our governess' bed-room, which opened out of it on the right overlooked a fine expanse of park, with azure tinted hills in the distance; our bedrooms were also close to Miss Varcoe's, my little apartment just separating my sister's from hers.

A servant called Mary Spank who was especially to attend us, also slept in a room of our wing, and at night we were perfectly secluded from the rest of the house by a large door at the end of our corridor, which was regularly barred and locked every night.

The first week passed over tolerably quiet with the exception that sundry hints of a future application of the rod in case of non-improvement were thrown out for our benefit.

Now our governess had told us that Monday was to be what she called "progress day," when we were to go over and repeat all we had learnt during the previous week.

So the first day of the second week found Miss Varcoe busily examining us as to what we retained in our minds. My sisters seemed to give some little cause for complaint, but when it came to my turn all the instructions of the previous six days seemed as it were to have gone in at one ear and out at the other.

"Percy, come here," at last exclaimed Miss Varcoe, taking me by the wrist and marching off towards her own room adjoining, "you have been so inattentive I must give you something to make you try to learn in future or you will be a disgrace to my teaching."

As she dragged me out of the schoolroom I could see my two

sisters tittering with delight, but my governess's dark flashing and compressed lips actually filled me with dread.

As we entered her bedroom I caught sight of a green-looking bunch of twigs neatly tied together with a red silk ribbon, which was lying on her bed.

"Now sir," she said seating herself on a broad low stool by the bedside, as she threw me across her lap, "your bottom shall smart a little, and if does no good, the next time I shall be much more severe."

In spite of my kicks and cries she soon had my breeches down to my heel and gave me about half-a-dozen good smacks with her hand on my sore bottom. This made me furious with rage and pain, so much so that I actually bit her thigh through her thin skirts.

"You little wretch," she screamed, "you bite, do you?" And reaching for the rod she wacked me with it till she was almost out of breath, and my bottom seemed cut to pieces.

"Bite again, will you?" she cried, gasping for breath.

"Oh—oh—oh—dear Miss Varcoe. I—I'll—never do it again, and learn my lessons too," I cried.

But all in vain, cut followed cut till at last the rod was worn to a stump and my cries had subsided into faint groans and sobs.

"Now Percy," say my governess, suddenly rising, "go to bed and stop there all day. I hope I've done you good, you bad boy. There, kiss me and say you will try and learn."

"Indeed, I will, Miss Varcoe," I cried, as she covered my burning cheeks with kisses seemingly agitated in a most strange manner and hugging me to her heaving bosom.

I had scarcely time to dry my tears and prepare to get into bed before I heard our governess's voice in her room again, this time evidently with one of my two sisters.

"Lady Emily," I heard her say, "your own conduct was almost as bad as Percy's, but to make fun of his punishment, fie—fie, you bad girl, you shall have something to laugh at."

My own pain was forgotten in a moment and I was at once eager to see my eldest sister punished. "What a lark," I thought to myself, as I crept up to the partially closed door, and found that I could see all that was going on in the next room without being observed.

Miss Varcoe was evidently in a great passion, as she was tying sister Emily's hands to the bedstead.

"Oh, dear lady, do forgive me this once, I'll never laugh again," piteously cried my sister.

"I don't think you will after I've let you feel the birch!" cries our governess.

I now saw her remove the bodice of her own dress, to allow more freedom to her arms, then slipping off her skirt, she pinned up her petticoats well above the knee, displaying to my sight her beautiful rounded bosom and legs, encased in red silk stockings.

I was too young then to be affected by the sight, but in after years it would have been most exciting.

Poor Emily's dress and petticoats were next pinned up over her shoulders, and the ruthless hands of Miss Varcoe next removed the drawers, and put the chemise out of the way, leaving my big sister's glorious fine fat bottom fully exposed to my view.

Another birch was taken from a drawer, and Miss Varcoe stood with it in her hand contemplating the fine expanse of white plump buttocks before her.

My sister looked the picture of indignation, her face and neck covered with crimson blushes, whilst the big tears coursed down her cheeks.

"How indelicate to be so exposed, its shameful, I'll tell Lady P.," she sobs.

"Your rude bottom must be disgraced if you don't know how to behave respectfully, and if you dare complain to her ladyship it will be worse still for you," cries Miss V., as she begins to exercise her skill on the naked flesh.

The cuts are smart and quick, causing the bottom of the culprit to wriggle at each stroke, it is a very wavy birch, and the tips of the twigs seem to go right round her thighs and buttocks at each stroke, and to my sight appeared to cut into even the most private places.

Deep red marks follow every stroke on the tender skin, and the victim fairly shrieks with pain.

"Mercy, oh, mercy, dear lady, I can't bear it, I shall die. Oh—oh ah, let me go!"

Miss Varcoe seems carried away by her fury, her lips are compressed and the dark eyes flash angrily as she unconsciously raises her clothes still more with her left hand, and not wearing drawers displays to my wondering sight a perfect forest of black hair hanging half way down between her thighs, and covering her white belly in dark bushy masses; the wandering hand gropes between her legs and is almost lost to sight.

"There, there, there," she cries, as she cuts more and more fiercely with the rod.

Poor Emily is almost fainting, and slight drops of blood trickle down her thighs as the flesh gets still more lacerated.

"Now will you tell Lady P.," cries Miss V., "such impudence."

"Oh—oh—dear, forgive—I'll never," screamed the victim.

Just at this moment the fierce appearance of Miss V.'s face gives place to a most pleased expression as her clothes are dropped and the right arm suddenly forgets to strike.

Dropping the remains of the birch she at once releases the poor girl, and giving mutual kisses of forgiveness, dismisses my poor bruised sister to the care of the servant, whilst I scuttle into bed for fear of discovery.

Once between the sheets my thoughts were so entranced and delighted by what I had seen that I soon fell asleep, and remained soundly oblivious of everything for several hours, till I was awakened by a smarting sensation as I felt a soft hand passed over my poor sore bum.

"Percy, dear, do you feel it much now," said a soft voice.

I opened my eyes to find it quite dark.

"Who is it?" I enquired.

"Only me, Miss Varcoe," said the voice, "you have slept so long you must want something to take."

"I am sore and hungry too," I said.

"Come into my room then, dear," she said, "you know I love

you too much to hurt you, if I was not obliged to do it for your good."

I was soon placed in her bed and regaled with some sandwiches and jellies, whilst Miss V. was undressing herself for the night, taking great care to conceal herself as much as possible from my sight during the operation.

At last putting out the light and getting into bed she says, "Percy you shall sleep with me to-night, dear," clasping me in her arms and covering me with kisses; the front of her nightdress was open, and I buried my face between the swelling globes of her bosom, kissing and hugging them in every possible way, whilst she amused herself by caressing every part of my naked body, her wandering touches not even excepting my little tiddler as she called it.

"I can't sleep," she said, "what a pity we can't play some game to tire us."

"Let's play at cows and calves," I exclaimed. "You kneel on all fours, I'll get under you and pretend to suck like a calf. I've often played it with my sisters."

"Very well," she said in a whisper, "only you must never tell any one," getting on her hands and knees, turning down the bed head foremost.

"Oh dear, Miss V.," I exclaimed, "what a lot of hair you have on your belly."

"That's nothing, Percy," she whispered, don't talk so loud, all grown-up women and men have hair there. You'll be the same when you get big."

I laid on my back and nestled my face in the long hair between her thighs, playing with the curls and kissing the soft lips of what she called her little cunny, which she pressed and rubbed down upon my face till I felt it getting very hot and suddenly wet, as at the same moment she pulled me away and buried her face between my thighs and tickling my tiddler with her lovely tongue, says, "you know the old cows are fond of licking their calves, so I must do it too."

"There, the game's over now," she continued, "we must go to sleep."

Miss Varcoe's terrible severity had such an effect upon us all, that it was nearly six months before the rod was required again.

My thoughts continually reverted to the game of cows and calves, and day by day I longed to pass another night with my beautiful hairy governess, till at last the idea occurred that if my bottom was sore again she might take pity on me as before.

Lady Bella, my youngest sister, was a spirited quick-tempered girl, and something tempted me that if I could only draw her into some scrape, I should have the additional pleasure of seeing her birched perhaps, as I had seen Emily.

Next afternoon in the schoolroom I was provided with a good sharp pin, and amused myself by slyly pricking her fat little bottom; each prick made her wince and look angrily at me, but the fear of our governess kept her quiet, but at last a vigorous thrust made her spring up and slap my face, exclaiming, "you nasty little wretch, take that if you won't leave me alone." Her temper was so excited, that had not Miss Varcoe at once interposed, she would have severely beaten me.

"What's all this fighting," exclaims our governess, seizing each of us by the arms.

"He's sticking pins in my bottom!" exclaimed Bella.

"It isn't true, Miss Varcoe," I said, pretending to look very innocent.

"You little story-teller," exclaims our governess "I saw you drop the pin, come to my room this instant, telling lies is worse than all, fine goings on I must say," dragging me after her.

"Now, my little lordling," she continued, when we got into her bedroom, "just slip down your trousers whilst I find a good birch."

She presently produced a fine bunch of twigs from a cupboard in the corner, and looking at me, exclaimed, "come here you bad boy," but I did not move, and made no effort to undress, her stern demeanour quite taking away all my courage.

I was now seized by the collar and dragged towards the stool by the bedside, but this time before laying me across her lap she carefully turned up her silk skirt and petticoats, displaying all her glory of fine legs and silk stockings. My trousers offer but feeble resistance to her impatient hands, and in trice my poor naked little bum feels the first smart of the rod.

Whisk—whisk—whisk, goes the birch, and my poor behind is cut in weals and bruises, quicker than I can relate.

"Dear, dear, Miss Varcoe," I scream, "do, do, have mercy, you'll kill me quite."

"Will you—will you—prick your sister's bottom with pins again," she cries, slashing away till at last quite exhausted she pitches away the rod, and giving me a rapturous kiss, "there, I hope I shall never have to do it again you bad boy, go to bed and stop there."

Crestfallen and smarting with pain I run to my own room, sobbing and forgetting all my aspirations; presently I hear our governess talking to but some one in her room.

"You bad tempered girl, lady Bella, I'm ashamed of you to fight your little brother," I heard her say.

The noise at once put me on the *qui vive* to see what was going on, and I softly stepped behind the partially closed door as so to look through the crack.

Poor Bella looked awfully frightened, as Miss V. held her by the wrist.

"You must be severely corrected for such hoydenish roughness, I can never overlook such temper," exclaims Miss V.

"Oh, pardon me this time, dear governess, you don't know how he stuck the pin into my bottom," cried my sister.

"No excuse at all," says Miss V. angrily, "I have severely punished Percy, and now you shall make the acquaintance with my birch."

Bella's dress is now removed, and Miss V. throwing off her bodice and skirt, looks terribly in earnest as she presses the poor girl down on the bed, so that her bottom projects well out over the edge, petticoats, chemise, and drawers are all put aside or removed, and my youngest sister presents quite a fine display of rounded buttocks and dimpled bum, I can even see the little rosy pouting slit between her legs as they are stretched well apart.

My fair governess gives the white globes a smarting smack, which brings a reddish tint all over the tender surface, and her look of rage increases as she takes the rod in hand.

Miss Varcoe now regardless of the shrieks and screams of her victim, applies the rod with furious vigour. "Yes, yes," she cries, "let me catch you striking any one again, and I'll cut you to pieces."

My sister's bottom is speedily a mass of weals and bruises, but the sight has a strange fascination for me, and I continue to feast my eyes upon the sight till Miss V. exhausts her fury, and almost falls over her fainting victim, who has really swooned under the agony of the punishment. Our governess' kisses fail to arouse the poor girl, who is carried insensible to her room, whilst I'm careful to get safe between my sheets.

Late in the evening Miss Varcoe takes me to her bed as before, where I am refreshed and caressed by her all night, since which I have played many a game of "cows and calves" between her lovely thighs, and revelled in the dark hairy precincts of her luscious cunny, and have grown to love the operation of the birch, as it invariably procured me the happiness of spending the night in her bed."

My dear Sir Charles, another day I will send you further extracts from his lordship's diary, and remain,

Yours to command,
ZOBEIDE NORTH.

CHAPTER IV.

Letter from Sir Charles Wildish to Mrs. North.

Dear Zobeide,

Your name appended to the epistle containing Lord P.'s early experience quite reminds me that I have often thought the Eastern's of olden times must have been thoroughly acquainted with the art of Erotic Flagellation! for instance your namesake in the Arabian Nights, who used to flog the three bitches and weep over them every evening, and at the present day we know it is generally practised by the worn out and effete monarchs of the harem.

Your relation of his lordship's adventure, makes me press you to send the sequel, if possible, as the recital terminated just were there seemed a prospect of most interesting results.

Presuming you will do your best to oblige me in this matter, I will reward you in anticipation by one or two little tales that I think will meet your approval, and be interesting to your friends.

Baboons, you know have fine bare backsides.

Well, some years ago a friend of mine conceived a sudden idea of keeping several of these animals for the purpose of adding to his lascivious amusements, and having procured four fine specimens, he had two commodious cages erected for them in his conservatory, placing two females in one, and another female with a rather elderly male in the second. For some time he used daily to watch their amorous dalliance, frigging and fucking, which procured him many a luscious treat in the arms of various female domestics, when he occasionally found them having a sly peep at the obscene beasts. At last poor Pongo, who was daily allowed to visit his two wives in the first cage, gave evident signs of slowness in his endeavours to please them, so much so that one frequently kept slapping his arse while he did best to fuck the other.

My friend, Mr. Buck, was highly delighted at this, and determined to give the baboon ladies a hint how better to get a rise out of their old man. Accordingly he got his confidential housekeeper to give him a good birching on a sofa in front of the animals, and then gave her a good fucking for them to see effect.

This so excited Mr. Pongo that he worked away nearly all day to please one or the other of his ladies, and next morning, after a couple of bouts with his sleeping partner, was quite done up, when Mr. B. allowed him to visit his second and third wives.

Now was the opportunity for trying the experiment, so Mr. B. at once offered a nice little birch to one of the females, who seized it with evident pleasure, grinning and whisking it about, chatting furiously all the while as the other was handling his limp prick and vainly trying to excite him.

Mr. Pongo seemed quite indifferent to these proceedings, and at last lazily stretched himself on the straw as if he intended to take a quiet nap before attempting any serious business, but his two ladyloves were not to be so put off, the one who had been softly feeling and frigging his old cock suddenly seized him by the head so as to hold him down, whilst the other with the birch at once commenced to soundly whip his posteriors with the rod.

Poor Pongo yelled with pain, but he had been taken at such a disadvantage, that all his efforts to rise or escape their fury were utterly useless.

His brownish white-looking arse was soon suffused with a blushing red, the sight of which only seemed to add to the fury of the ladies; whilst one plied the rod with might and main, the other tried to help by thrashing his prick with a wisp of straw.

Such a novel blood stirring had the desired effect in a very few minutes, and poor Pongo's red-headed priapus stood ready to burst which excitement.

After having slightly allayed the raging lust of his females, Mr. B. also supplied him with a rod, when with evident gusto he fairly repaid them for their erotic kindness.

I was one of the favoured few Mr. B. occasionally allowed to witness this exhibition of monkey birch discipline, so I can truthfully vouch for its being a correct statement of the fact.

In India, at the present day, the obscenities of the Brahmin worship of Vishnu are notorious; the Nautch girls dance most lasciviously in order to excite the male worshippers to copulate with them, and such as are elderly or not easily excited by their wanton motions, are seized by the girls and beaten with bunches of green bamboos till they are in a fit state for the necessary sacrifice to the Heathen Deity.

A late noble Lord Chancellor once resided in a semidetached house at Wimbledon, and had for his next-door neighbour a Mrs. Thornton, who kept a select ladies' school, not more than a dozen pupils, fine well grown girls from twelve to eighteen, mostly the daughters of parents residing abroad.

Mr. S., as the then future Chancellor was called, was often disturbed in his rest by the laughter, singing, or other noises made by the young ladies in their bedrooms at night. So, one night, being out of patience after a restless night, he knocked at the door and sent his card in to Mrs. T.

The servant ushered him into the front drawing-room, where the lady of the house speedily came to enquire the reason of her being honoured by a call.

"Ah—ahem," exclaims the bashful barrister, who quite loses his forensic coolness in the presence of the grand-looking schoolmistress. "The fact is—is—Madam, I'm sorry to say its quite impossible for me to get my necessary rest. Your young ladies often make such a noise just as I want to fall asleep after a hard day's work. Were you not a home last night, Madam?"

"Ah, I suppose when the cat's away the mice will play. I went to the Italian Opera in London last night," replies Mrs. T., "but, sir, they will sing a different tune this evening if my suspicions are confirmed."

"My dear Madam," stammered Mr. S., "pray don't punish them on my account, I only thought you would hint to them that they are heard in the next house, and so give them a caution about the noise."

"Certainly, sir," exclaims Mrs. T., with a lively twinkle in her piercing eyes, "but my hints are cautions duly administered on their posteriors with a good birch rod, so you will no doubt excuse a little screeching this evening."

"By God, madam," cries S., "I'd rather be birched myself than have those dear lovely girls hurt."

"No substitutes are admissible," says Mrs. T. "The good behaviour of the whole establishment is at stake, doubtless you were birched when you went to school, Mr. S., were you not?"

"Yes, indeed, madam, I've a most lively remembrance of it, our master's hand was heavy, but to be birched by your elegant hand must be lovely, what would I not give to see the scene?" he exclaimed.

"It's not to be thought of, Mr. S.," says the lady, "it would disgrace my house if known."

"Madam," exclaims he, "you know I'm a man of the law who seldom sees any amusements, this idea tickles my fancy so, I will give you fifty guineas for a sight this once, it could easily be managed without fear of discovery."

The offer was too tempting to be refused, but Mrs. T. expresses her horror of such a thing, and only gave way to his repeated pressing of the subject, "because she knew there could be no harm with such a respectable steady gentleman."

"Only this once, I'll never consent to it again," said Mrs. T., as he pressed her when taking his leave.

Accordingly Mr. S. again makes his appearance about seven o'clock in the evening, and is at once secretly conducted by Mrs. T. to her little study, which communicates with the schoolroom by means of a glass door, a thin red curtain covers the glass to a considerable height, and the upper panes being removed for purposes of ventilation, a listener can hear all that passed in the room beyond.

"Now be careful," whispers Mrs. T., "this room is in darkness, and by slipping aside a corner of the curtain you can see all without being observed."

Mr. S. is transported with the arrangement, and kissing her hand places the crisp bank notes in her grasp, whispers in return, "Now make haste, madam, I am all impatience, and let the exhibition be as free as you can."

"Thank you," says Mrs. T., as she locks him in, and Mr. S. at once slips off his boots for fear of making any noise, and cautiously draws a little bit of the red curtain aside, so as to get a complete view of all in the schoolroom.

There are eleven young ladies, besides the English and French governesses, and judging by the anxious looks of two or three, serious business seems impending.

After a short delay, Mrs. T. makes her appearance, and taking her seat at a desk in the centre of the room which stands on a slightly raised platform, clears her throat with a preparatory—hem.

"Miss Smithson," she says, "you're the senior governess, and ought to keep order in my absence, how is it that I have complaints of noise in the young ladies' room at night, from the quiet old gentleman next door?"

"Please, madam," replies the English governess, "I severely reprimanded the young ladies who sleep in No. I room last night; I was asleep, but went to them the instant I heard the noise, and found a grand battle going on with pillows and bolsters for fun, and certainly should have reported it to you but for their tearful promises never to do so again."

"Misses Grey, Ellis, and Shaw, stand up, for such conduct cannot be overlooked, you are the oldest girls in the school, and ought to know better," says Mrs. T., looking very cross.

One blushing girl, a beautiful blonde with blue eyes, instantly seized by the French governess, a strong, swarthy woman with a relentless expression of countenance.

"Oh, Mrs. Thornton, spare me, forgive us this once," cries the frightened girl, who is at least seventeen.

"Miss Grey, you're the oldest, make haste and prepare her, Mdlle. Cadeau," exclaims Mrs. T.

Assisted by two of the young ladies, the English governess brings forward one of the desks, which, covered with green baize, has a sloping top at each side, one end is tilted up by being put upon a stool, whilst the other inclines towards the glass door of the private study.

Poor Miss Grey is dumb with confusion, her face crimson with indignation, as she passively submits to her dress being slipped off.

The two governesses next hoist her upon the desk, but the spirited young lady suddenly awakens from her lethargy, and upsets Cadeau by a desperate kick; however her struggles are in vain, as by the assistance of the other young ladies (who seem quite to anticipate a treat), her legs are secured and tied on each side, whilst her body lies all along the top ridge of the desk, the victim's arms being held on either side by the governesses.

The whiteness of her flesh is beautifully set off by the green covering of the desk she is horsed upon, and as her splendid buttocks are uncovered by the necessary turning up and securing of her petticoats, chemise, &c., Mr. S. can plainly see the rosy pouting lips of her virgin slit, beautifully fringed by darker hair than might be expected.

Mrs. T. now takes a fine birch rod from the desk, and descends from her seat.

"I hope," she says, "the punishment of these young ladies will have a good effect on the whole school."

Standing a little on one side, so as not at all to obstruct the view, she poises the birch and well measures the distance.

Her strokes at first are rather light, till warming to her work, they grow fast and furious. Miss Grey's fine posteriors soon begin to look red and inflamed, each blow adding to the fiery colour of the exposed bottom.

The girl shows great courage, not a whimper escapes her

compressed lips, but tears of agony are visible as they course down the flushed cheeks.

Some of the blows mercilessly cut through her tender thighs, and turn the rosy tint of her secret charms to a deep vermillion.

Whisk—whisk, fall the blows with unabated fury, till the poor girl writhes and rubs her hairy mount upon the ridge, and at last goes off in a swoon, which does not at all appear to be painful, but the result of some very pleasing emotion.

"There, let her down, and make haste with the other two," cries Miss T., as she excitedly throws aside the worn-out rod.

Misses Ellis and Shaw, two fair girls about fifteen or sixteen, are now brought to the front, the former a fine stout strongly built girl, struggles violently to prevent her dress being removed, and is with some difficulty horsed on the desk, her flashing eyes and blushing cheeks showing her excitement as she exclaims to her schoolfellows, who are helping to secure her restive limbs: "Ah, ah—wait, girls, till your time comes, won't I help to secure you!"

Miss Shaw is a slender timid girl; and offers no resistance, she is soon horsed and straddling over Miss Ellis's back, so that both bottoms show one just over the other, a most enchanting scene of well-developed plump white arses, white fleshy thighs, and beautiful legs in silk stockings and elegant Balmoral boots.

"Mdlle. Cadeau," exclaims Mrs. T., "I'm quite exhausted, do you take this birch, and give those naughty bottoms a lesson they won't soon forget."

The dark-faced Frenchwoman's eyes sparkled with delight as she takes the rod in hand, and at once commences to give them a taste of her proficiency.

Her strokes do not seem so very hard, but are so cunningly delivered, that the tips of the birch seem to search out and sting the most tender parts. Now and again a good whacking cut comes right across their buttocks, causing deep red marks and weals, but it is the poor pouting red lips of the virgin cunnies and the inner surfaces of their thighs which most feel the smart.

They scream for mercy in chorus, and twist about in agony;

no one pities them. Miss Grey, who is quite recovered from her swoon, looks evidently pleased, and the others all seem without feeling as they look on with flushed cheeks and sparkling eyes.

Not till the poor girls go off in delirious agony is any mercy shown, and then they are let down, and in company with Miss Grey, are hurried off to bed, where they console each other's wounded feelings in mutual loving and amorous dalliance, till they fall asleep to dream it all over again.

Mr. S. has been a most excited observer all through the scene, his steady-going old pego is almost ready to burst, as the lights being extinguished in the schoolroom, Mrs. T. unlocks the door to release him.

"I hope, sir, you have enjoyed your novel idea," she whispers. "You must go now."

"No, no. Madam," he cries, "you must first punish me for my nasty thoughts in wishing to see such a sight," and at the same time putting his arm round her waist, he draws her to his side on a sofa behind the door.

"You bad man, as if I would do such a thing," she exclaims.

"But I won't go till you do," he replies; "and you can't help yourself," placing her hand on his excited cock, which he has released from his trousers. "And I mean to make you so angry you will be sure to do it in a rage," he continued, throwing her back on the sofa, glueing his lips to hers, and at the same time putting his hand under her clothes, and by a rapid march (as a soldier would say) surprising the enemy in a wet and excited state, quite unprepared, to withstand the bold attack.

With a sigh her legs give way, and his rampant battering ram is presented to the breach; he shoves, she shrinks, but comes again with an unexpected heave of her buttocks, burying the assailant in a hot gushing flood of sperm, as he is engulphed up to the hilt; this so excites Mr S., that a very few thrusts are sufficient to complete his share of the business.

Mrs. T. clings convulsively to her ravisher, but all the luscious throbbing and nipping of her vagina fail to keep Mr. Priapus in his place, he gets suddenly limp and loses his position.

"You wicked man," whispers the lady, "how have you taken advantage of my defenceless position. I could indeed thrash you now."

"Do, do, dear Madam. My brutal conduct deserves correction," replied Mr. S., eagerly.

"I think I will," says Mrs. T. "There's enough light from the moon to see what I'm about; and a good fresh birch still in my desk in the schoolroom."

No sooner said than done, and in a minute or two, she is again seated on the sofa, with the gentleman on his knees before her kissing the rod.

"Now sir," she says, "your bottom shall smart for your impudent rudeness."

"Oh—mercy—forgive," whimpers Mr, S. "I'll never take such liberties again."

"Get up, sir," she says, sharply, "and lay across my lap, or it will be worse for you," and she raises her skirts and petticoats so as to put him across her naked thighs, but S. again seizes the opportunity, and thrusting his head under her clothes, covers her belly, thighs, and hairy mount with rapturous kisses.

"You wretch," she exclaims, "you get worse and worse in your obscenity," and strenuously exerting herself at last pulls him on to her lap, his trousers being still undone, she soon bares his posterior and thighs almost to the knees.

Placing her left around his body and under the belly, so as to hold him securely, she at once cuts away in fury, exclaiming:

"My learned sir, your buttocks shall feel a punishment you have little idea of."

Whack—whack—whack, goes the rod, wealing poor S.'s arse at every stroke, and almost taking his breath away. He groans and writhes in the most intense agony.

"My good Madam, stop, stop," he cries, "the books I've read made me anticipate a pleasing sensation, but this is horrible," grinding his teeth.

"So you've been reading obscene books, have you, you dirty old fellow, and then get up your tales about my young ladies to gratify your lust," she at once exclaimed, if possible striking harder still.

Just at this moment of excitement, S.'s prick is so revived, that she spasmodically grasps it in her hand, and thinking only of her own wants, relaxes her blows, so that the previous torture turns to a beautiful exciting heat, and he wriggles about upon her naked thighs in a most lascivious manner.

Thus ended S.'s first birching, and after another amorous fuck, this time prolonged by their proper appreciation of the enjoyment, they separate most lovingly.

For four years Mrs. T. indulged Mr. S.'s penchant for the rod, till at last, failing to inveigle him into a marriage, she made an advantageous match and left Mr. S. to cater for himself in future.

This letter is so long, pray excuse my not referring to personal experience, dear Zobeide,

Ever yours with the birch,
C. WILDISH.

CHAPTER V.

Letter from Mrs. North to Sir Charles Wildish.

Dear Sir Charles,

Your last letter was so especially interesting that it is only fair I should try to amuse you in return, and fortunately I can send you some more extracts from Lord P.'s diary; how he would have enjoyed the perusal of your letters.

You will not thank me much for reflections, so shall go on with the diary once more.

"This continued for a long time till my thirteenth birthday was passed, when one day after my sisters had left the schoolroom Miss Varcoe, kissing me very tenderly, said, "Percy, dear, what makes you so naughty, you have to be birched more than ever now, and yet you make good progress in your studies, how is it?"

"Dear, Miss Varcoe," I replied, my whole heart leaping as it were towards her, "I love you so, and your birching gives me such pleasure I cannot describe, if you would do it without my being naughty I should always be good."

My governess's face flushed scarlet, but her eyes too plainly told her languishing desire.

"Dear boy," she exclaims, drawing me on her lap, "what should you feel to make you wish for pain?"

"My kind governess," I whispered, throwing my arms round

her neck, "at first it smarts terribly, but that soon goes off, and I feel such a delicious throbbing warmth,—but I can't tell you, I should like to be always in bed with you."

"Why, Percy, what do you mean, you bad boy?" she laughingly said, her cheeks crimsoning again, "you like that game we play, do you?"

"It's so nice, I can't help it," I whispered again, "and lovely to cuddle and kiss your hairy belly, and I feel ready to die when you kiss my little thing."

We sat kissing and hugging for some time, and I felt one of her hands gradually inserted as she undid the front of my trousers, till at last my little cock was being handled and caressed by her soft fingers, causing him soon to feel hard and stiff.

"Percy, dear," she says softly," is that what you like, shall I kiss it now?"

"Oh, do—do—," I said eagerly, "it's so beautiful to feel your tongue on it."

Seating me in the chair she knelt in front, at the same time fully exposing and uncovering the ruby head of my little swelling affair, then closing her cherry lips upon it, her tongue rolled round and round, the sucking and titillation giving me the most intense delight, I soon felt ready to burst. Exclaiming, "Oh, you darling, Miss Varcoe, how nice I feel—I don't know what—pray—pray—keep on kissing it," thinking she was going to stop.

Just then my cock seemed bigger and stiffer than ever and with a palpitating heave, something lumpy seemed to shoot from my balls as she tickled them right along the urinal passage into her mouth.

The exquisite throbbing sensation continued for a few seconds, then a slight oblivious fainting as I closed my eyes in extacy, and convulsively pressed her head down as if she was not yet near enough.

Presently I felt her hot kisses on my mouth as she murmured, "Percy, dear, tell me you're all right, I'm afraid you might be hurt," at the same time her hand caressed and settled my now limp little affair, and comfortably buttoned me up again.

"Oh, what have I done? What did I do in your mouth?" I exclaimed, coming to myself.

"Be quiet now, dear," she whispers, "you shall sleep with me every night, and I can tell you all about it in bed."

She now left me, and I waited with impatience for bedtime, my hour for retiring was eight o'clock, but it was fully two hours before I heard Miss Varcoe enter her bedroom, when I at once jumped up and rushed to her without waiting to be fetched.

"Fie—fie—Percy," she exclaimed, suddenly raising my night-shirt, and exposing the rampant state of my little cock at the same time grasping and squeezing it tenderly, "why it's as hard as iron, but you naughty boy, see, I have a fine rod for such an impudent fellow."

"You did not expect this," she continued, throwing me on the bed face downwards, and turning my only garment almost over my head, leaving all the back, bottom, and thighs at the mercy of the rod.

She quite terrified me, so in earnest did she look, with flashing eyes and heaving bosom; but I had no time for reflection, the birch commenced in rapid cuts, and travelled all over my back down to the lower thighs, each stroke rather slowly delivered, leaving me in painful uncertainly where the next would fall.

The suddenness of her attack made me quite furious at being thrashed for nothing.

"You monster," I hissed between my teeth, "is this your sort of love, only give me the chance to serve you the same."

"What a change in a few short hours," she exclaimed, pitilessly; "from darling love to monster."

Back, ribs, and loins, as well as thighs and buttocks, were being literally cut to pieces, and I felt it would make me sore for a week at least, but—

Whack—whack—whisk, continued the birch on my poor bottom without mercy, until I almost died away, shooting again something thick into her hand, which had just been placed on my stiff cock to feel how it was.

She at the same time seemed to tremble all over in some indefinable way, and dropping the worn out rod, sank by my side on the bed.

Recovering herself, I was placed between the sheets as comfortable as possible, and the curtains drawn to prevent my peeping as she prepared herself to retire.

In a few minutes the lights were extinguished, and as she settled herself by my side, I could not resist throwing my arms round her neck and rapturously kissing her, whispered: "Oh, I love you more than ever now, dear governess."

"Percy, we must go to sleep now," she replies, returning my caress, "or it will be too much for one day."

"What do you mean? dear Miss Varcoe," I enquired. "Why may we not have a game now we're in bed?"

"I suppose I must explain," she says. "Percy have you ever felt anything come from your stiff little thing before to-day. You know what I mean?"

"No, dear governess, what could it be?" I whispered, bashfully. "Never before have I felt so excited, and the delicious sensation you caused me with your tongue. Ah! it was quite heavenly."

"Well, then, dear," she goes on, "you are getting a man now, and what you ejected into my mouth and hand was the seed of life, which, when it passes into the womb of a woman, causes the babies to come."

"But where is the womb, and how does it get in?" I asked.

"There," she says, "what do you call this?" patting my still stiff little affair with her hand.

"Well," I replied, "boys call it a cock, tiddler, or diddle."

"Your cock, then, must find its way into a woman in the slit between her legs, and eject the seed there to make a baby," she continued.

"Have you ever had it done to you, dear Miss Varcoe?" I asked.

"Oh dear no," she exclaimed; "I dare not, all I know is learnt from a book; but there is another way we may do without risk, but not to night, as it may injure your health to make an ejection too often, it is so weakening to one so young.

"My dear governess, how kind of you to explain all this to me; but to change the subject, I wish you would sometimes birch

Emily or Bella, I should so like to peep and see it done. Do tell me when you are going to do it?" I said.

"You young rogue," she whispered, squeezing me to her bosom, and covering my mouth with hot kisses, "you will grow to live on the birch. Do you know it is the greatest pleasure I have, to expose and well thrash a pretty bottom, but a beautiful boy is much better than a girl to my taste."

"What do you think?" she whispered; "only it's a great secret, I am almost certain there is something between Bob, your mamma's page, and our Mary; if I could but catch them, their bottoms shall add to our pleasure."

This ended the conversation, and we were soon lost in balmy sleep, and oblivious of all but the influence of sweet dreams.

I awoke in the morning in the midst of a beautiful vision of Miss V. sucking and caressing my cock, which was as hard as iron, and the tip all moist and clammy, but my sweet bedfellow had already vanished.

During the day, after luncheon, Miss V. whispered to me, "glorious news, you know I was up early, and it so happened, going to Mary's room to call her, found Master Buttons fast asleep in her arms, this evening, when they come into the school-room for their usual lesson, which, you know, Lady P. asked me to be so good as to give them, three times a week, they will have to pay for their games, so be ready for the fun, my dear."

At seven o'clock the two unsuspecting culprits duly put in their appearance for an expected hour's schooling.

"Percy, stop here," exclaimed Miss Varcoe, as I was about to retire from the room with my sisters, "I want to speak to you."

Emily and Bella looked round with surprise, but were soon gone, and Miss V., stepping to the door, locked and bolted it, besides placing the back of a chair so no one could lock through the keyhole.

Seating herself in an armchair and motioning me to a seat close by, she said sternly, "Where did you sleep last night, Robert?"

The boy's face turned crimson, whilst Mary was pale and red by turns. Bob was silent.

"Perhaps you will answer for him, Mary,?" asked Miss V., casting one of her most penetrating looks on the confused girl. No answer.

"At least," said Miss V. sharply, "I'm glad you don't add falsehood to your other fault, I should not wish you to lose your places, but you must both be severely punished for your indecent conduct, I saw you in each others arms this morning, and Mary must have unbolted the door to admit Robert, as you know I always see to the bolts myself before I retire at night."

"Miss Varcoe," cried Mary, sinking on her knees, "it shall never happen again, besides, Bob is my cousin, and always used to sleep with me at home; oh, pray miss, don't, oh don't tell my lady, anything rather than that."

"Unless I punish you both severely, I must tell lady P. It is my duty," exclaims Miss Varcoe, "or shall I birch you both?"

"We would rather submit to you, dear Miss," they both said at once.

"Then, here's the rod," replies Miss V. sternly.

"Percy, help Mary to lay Robert on that desk, and take down his trousers and tuck up his shirt."

"Oh, Miss," exclaims Bob, "that's so indecent, any-how, but on my bare bottom."

"Why Mary's seen it lots of times, and Percy is a boy like yourself, no more nonsense now," says Miss V.

Much as he dislikes it we soon extend him along the ridge of the desk, I undo his braces, whilst Mary kindly unbuttons his front and, I fancied, gave a loving caress to his cock as she pretended to pull up his shirt.

"Hold his legs as soon as you have tied his hands down," said Miss V., flourishing a fine big birch.

"Now, my boy," she said, as soon as we were ready, "let me catch you sleeping with Mary again in our wing of the mansion."

Saying this, she poised the rod, and brought it down smartly on his fine white backside, then again and again each time increasing the force of her blows, large red weals are soon visible all over his previously white flesh.

Poor Bob is in agony, and twists himself about so, as each stroke makes him smart, that the spring of his fine fat bottom shows his finely developed cock and appendages, just beginning to be feathered with soft downy hair.

As I hold one leg this is the centre of attraction for me, and I watch the first gradual rise of his fine cock. At first limp, it soon begins to stiffen and hold up its head, till I could see the red vermillion tip rubbing itself, and ready to burst on the red baize of the desk.

Miss V. I also thought seemed much attracted by the same powerful magnet, but her blows did not yet relax, and she kept counting one, two, three, to the stroke for a minute or two, the fine bum before her being more and more cut up at each blow.

Presently poor Bob, who shows great pluck, seems to quite forget himself, and exclaims, "Oh,—oh,—ah, I'm coming, I can't help it," and laying almost in an insensible state on the desk, I cannot see his cock at all as it is hidden by his belly.

Miss V. also trembles all over in the same way I had previously observed the night before, her eyes expressing the most intense delight, and we are ordered to let him go at once; the door is unlocked, and he is told to be off.

Locked in again, we turn to the desk, when I at once perceived a very mysterious little puddle of some thick and gelatinous looking stuff on the top of the desk, just where Master Bob's cock had been, but almost as soon as I had noticed it, Mary wiped it away with her handkerchief.

"Now, Mary," says our governess, "it's your turn now, and I've no time to lose, just lay yourself over the end of the desk, Percy will tie your hands and pin up your clothes."

"La, oh, miss, I'm ashamed for him to see me," said Mary, a fine blooming girl of about eighteen, with reddish brown hair and rosy cheeks, all on fire from the excitement of Bob's birching.

"You need not mind him, he is not quite so old as Robert, who has no doubt long ago seen all you had to show, Mary," said Miss.

Saying which, she helped me to push the girl on to the desk, and with a good cord I secured her hands, one on either side, by passing it under the desk, from wrist to wrist.

Her feet just rested on the ground, and as we lifted the skirts and petticoats, what a glorious view was presented to our sight, one of the broadest and softest bottoms I ever saw, of the whitest possible flesh, well set off by beautiful swelling thighs, which, as she stood with her legs wide apart, fully exposed the pouting vermillion lips of a largish gap, well covered with blackish brown hair in great profusion, and set off, topped up as it were, by a good view of her dark brown bottom-hole, which had quite a fringe of hair around it.

We tied her legs to two heavy chairs, so as to keep them as they were, well apart, then Miss Varcoe, arming herself with a fine new birch.

"Mary Spank," she says, "how could you be so wicked as to take that boy to your bed," giving me an arch smile, "you are far the worst and oldest of the two, in fact you must have seduced him."

"No, indeed miss I didn't, he's such a rude, bold boy, he had sneaked into my room and hidden under the bed before you went your rounds," cried Mary. "Oh, I—oh, couldn't help it," she screams, as the first sharp cut makes her bum wince.

"I don't believe a word you say," exclaims Miss Varcoe, giving anther stinging cut, "don't add lies to your other bad ways. Didn't you seduce him, now?" giving a tremendous whack. "I believe you did, he was quite an innocent boy when he came here two months ago." Another and another heavy cut, causing the marks and weals to spread all over her bottom. "I could cut you to pieces, I could, you bad young woman, to seduce a boy like that," she cries.

"Mercy—mercy. Oh, I can't bear it," screams Mary.

"Spank you are, and spanked you'll be," says Miss Varcoe, furiously, and getting more and more in a rage. "Will you ever let him in again? I've a great mind now to ask Lady P. to get rid of you at once."

"Dear—dear miss, never, oh—oh—never will I let him in again, it was all through larking and playing. Oh—oh, I shall die," screams the victim.

The poor fat bottom is getting very raw and more cut up every moment, but Miss V. relaxes slightly in the fury of her blow, and glancing significantly towards me, directs her cuts so as to touch up the tender surfaces between her extended thighs, each stroke leaving its red mark, and reaching even to the now fiery lips of her mossy love grot.

Writhing with most acute pain, she did not scream again, but twisted and tried to squeeze her legs together, as she sighed and groaned by turns, till at last she seemed to lay on the desk almost inanimate and lost to further feeling, whilst I could perceive some considerable moisture exuding from her luscious gap.

Miss V. dropped the rod, and let down her clothes, unloosed both legs and arms, and giving her a shake, she opened her eyes dreamily, exclaiming: "Oh—oh—where am I? What a delightful feeling."

"Your bottom will be delightfully sore, if that's what you mean," said Miss V. "Now go to bed, and don't let me have cause to punish either of you again."

As soon as Mary was gone, Miss V. turned to me. "Percy dear," she said, kissing me with great warmth, "it's your bed time, I shan't be longer than I can help, this birching has excited me more than ever for a game with my dear boy." Scarcely an hour elapsed before, pleading a severe headache, she excused herself to my lady mother, with whom she was to pass evening, and hastened to rejoin me as I lay impatiently awaiting her.

"Come on, Percy," she said, in a low voice, as soon as she had secured the door, "you may help to undress me if you promise to behave yourself."

"Of course I will," I exclaimed, delighted at the idea, and almost as quick as thought I was at her side, pouting my lips for a kiss.

"You dear boy," she said, pressing her lips to mine, "let me first undress you, feeling is not sufficient, I must see your beautiful youthful figure to-night," and as quickly as I can write it, she removed my nightdress; "there now, help me, we can admire each other afterwards."

Her dress was soon removed, and next I unlaced her corset, setting free the firm round globes of her bosom, which I rapturously kissed, then next the petticoats are loosened, and she seats herself on a chair, whilst I remove her silk stockings, taking advantage of her position to give a sly kick to my excited little cocky, which I repaid by hot burning kisses on her legs and thighs. "Leave off, sir, a serious business has to be attended to," she said laughing, and was soon seated on a china utensil, delighting me with the noise of a mighty fall of water.

Tossing off her chemise we stand lovingly before the cheval glass, and I survey her charms with extacy, the regular features now lighted up with a fascinating smile, the dark languishing loving eyes, her beautifully plump rounded figure, marble white skin so finely contrasted with the flowing dark hair falling over her lovely shoulders, the slight moustache, and especially the forest of love lower down, covering all her belly from the navel downwards, such a luxuriance as I have never seen since, all which added to her fine thighs, calves, and small feet, almost made me doubt my senses, as we lovingly caressed each other.

"My beautiful boy; my Adonis," she whispered, carrying me to the bed, "you may think me immodest, but this was a temptation I couldn't resist, my life, my honour; everything I trust to you."

"I shall never think that," I replied, as we lay on the bed; "lovers can never see too much of each other."

"We have always played at cows and calves," she said, "but to-night you must be a young bull, you know how they mount on the cows' backs in the park sometimes;" then kneeling over me and lubricating my swelling cock in her mouth, she continued, "Now, my dear love mount behind." As I did so she applied a little cold cream from a box under the pillow, to her tight looking bottom-hole, and with her hand directed the head of my pego to the small orifice, saying, "Now push, dear, firmly and gently, you will soon get in."

My excitement was so great that I eagerly obeyed her directions, shoving and forcing my affair gradually further and further, till my balls shook against her bottom, my being so small it was easily done.

"Move gently in and out" she said, "we may safely enjoy ourselves this way, shooting your seed into my bottom can do no harm, it is only in the other place, there is risk of getting children."

She wriggled her bottom most wantonly, and drawing my arms around her waist, taught me to add to her pleasure.

Three times that night we repeat our sacrifice to love, each time swimming in a flood of delight, and the lesson my dear governess then taught me has never been forgotten."

Dear Sir Charles, I think this will be enough of Lord P.'s diary, the rest is too filthy for me to write.

So please excuse, and I am yours to birch when you please.

ZOBEIDE NORTH.

END OF VOL. II

BIRCHGROVE PRESS
Flagellant & Libertine Literature

Birchgrove Press specializes in producing new print and e-book editions of pre-1950s writings on sexual flagellation in English. Original editions of many of the books that we offer are difficult to obtain and are highly sought after. We are especially proud to offer new editions of rare Victorian flagellant texts such as *The Mysteries of Verbena House*, *Experimental Lecture by Colonel Spanker*, and *The Quintessence of Birch Discipline*. Birchgrove Press also produces new editions of libertine literature. We have published *Venus in the Cloister*, *The School of Venus*, *The Dialogues of Luisa Sigea*, and Isidore Liseux's translation of the Marquis de Sade's *Justine* (1791), *Opus Sadicum*, for example.

www.birchgrovepress.com

More books from
Birchgrove Press

The Convent School, or Early Experiences of a Young Flagellant.
First published in 1879. Includes its companion volume,
Miss Coote's Confession - two classic Victorian flagellant
novellas in one book.

*The Mysteries of Verbena House; or, Miss Bellasis Birched
for Thieving* - First published as two volumes in one in
1882.

Experimental Lecture by Colonel Spanker - One of the most
notorious English flagellant novellas. First published
in 1878-79. Includes *The Yellow Room,* first published 1891.

*The Pleasures of Cruelty; Being a sequel to the reading of
Justine et Juliette by the Marquis de Sade* - first published
as three volumes in one in 1886.

*Swivia; or, the Briefless Barrister. The Extra Special Number of
The Pearl* - first reprint in over a century of the 1879
Christmas edition of *The Pearl: A Journal of Facetiæ
and Voluptuous Reading* (1879-1880).

The Haunted House or The Revelations of Theresa Terence - first
reprint in over a century of the 1880 Christmas edition of
the *The Pearl: A Journal of Facetiæ and Voluptuous Reading*
(1879-1880).

The Romance of Chastisement; or, Revelations of the School and Bedroom. - Written by St. George H. Stock. First published 1871.

The Flogging-Block An Heroic Poem in a Prologue and Twelve Eclogues by Algernon Charles Swinburne. A Transcription of The Original Holograph Manuscript Written at intervals between 1862 and 1881 - first publication of Swinburne's mock-heroic tribute to corporal punishment.

The Whippingham Papers - first published 1887. Most of the pieces were written by St. George H. Stock. Includes poems by Swinburne.

Raped on the Railway A True Story of a Lady who was First Ravished and then Chastised on the Scotch Express - first published in Paris in 1899.

*The Petticoat Dominant or Woman's Revenge The Autobiography
of a Young Nobleman as a Pendant to Gynecocracy by
M. Le Comte du Bouleau.* First published 1898.

*Gynecocracy. A narrative of the Adventures and Psychological
Experiences of Julian Robinson (afterwards Viscount
Ladywood) Under Petticoat-Rule, written by himself.*
First published in 1893.

*Stays and Gloves: Figure-Training and Deportment
by Means of the Discipline of Tight Corsets,
Narrow High-Heeled Boots, Clinging Kid Gloves,
Combinations, etc., etc.* First published in 1909.

*White Stains The Literary Remains of George Archibald
Bishop a Neuropath of the Second Empire.*
Written by magician and occultist Aleister Crowley.
First published 1898.

Snowdrops from a Curate's Garden.
Written by Aleister Crowley. First published 1904.

Miss Mary - English translation of a French flagellant
   novel written by Alphonse Momas. First published 1907.

Miss Grégor - English translation of a French flagellant
   novel written by Alphonse Momas. First published 1907.

Whipping as a Fine Art - Edwardian flagellant novel
   attributed to Charles Sackville. First published c. 1909

*Les Mystères de la Maison de la Verveine: ou Miss Bellasis
   fouettée pour vol* - French translation of *The Mysteries
   of Verbena House*. First published in 1901. Facsimile edition.
.

The Exhibition of Female Flagellants: Parts One and Two -
Two volumes in one. First published c. 1780 - 1785.

Alraune - English translation of Hanns Heinz Ewers'
decadent novel. First published in German in 1911.

www.ingramcontent.com/pod-product-compliance
Lightning Source LLC
Chambersburg PA
CBHW070603180626
46817CB00005B/1975